"You've been living in a dream, Davina!"

Jake turned away in frustration as he continued, "Your saintly Philip isn't real! He may be your ex-fiancé, but he's a figment of your fantasies."

"How do you know what he's like?" Davina snapped. "You don't know him at all—" Her voice broke off raggedly. Then she went on, "And how dare you talk to me like this! You don't know anything about me or what I feel."

Jake was controlling his temper with difficulty. "Dreams are safe, but they're lifeless and cold." His eyes narrowed speculatively. "Perhaps it's time to bring you out of the clouds."

Before she could protest he had snatched her roughly to him, fastening his mouth on hers in a searing kiss.

WELCOME
TO THE WONDERFUL WORLD
OF *Harlequin Presents*

Interesting, informative and entertaining,
each Harlequin romance portrays an appealing
and original love story. With a varied array
of settings, we may lure you on an African safari,
to a quaint Welsh village, or an exotic Riviera
location—anywhere and everywhere that adventurous
men and women fall in love.

As publishers of Harlequin romances, we're
extremely proud of our books. Since 1949,
Harlequin Enterprises has built its publishing
reputation on the solid base of quality and
originality. Our stories are the most popular
paperback romances sold in North America; every
month, six new titles are released and sold at
nearly every book-selling store in Canada and the
United States.

A free catalogue listing all available Harlequin romances
can be yours by writing to the

HARLEQUIN READER SERVICE,
(In the U.S.) M.P.O. Box 707, Niagara Falls, N.Y. 14302
(In Canada) Stratford, Ontario, Canada N5A 6W2

We sincerely hope you enjoy reading
this Harlequin Presents.

Yours truly,

THE PUBLISHERS

SUSAN ALEXANDER

wedding in the family

Harlequin Books

TORONTO • LONDON • LOS ANGELES • AMSTERDAM
SYDNEY • HAMBURG • PARIS • STOCKHOLM • ATHENS • TOKYO

Harlequin Presents edition published May 1982
ISBN 0-373-10499-5

Original hardcover edition published in 1981
by Mills & Boon Limited

CHAPTER ONE

DAVINA turned out the lights and closed the office door firmly behind her. The slim gold watch on her wrist registered six-thirty, and she heaved a deep sigh of relief. After weeks of late-night working her first free evening stretched ahead, and she thought with longing of the hot bath and supper in front of the television she had promised herself.

Ignoring the open doors of the lift, she decided to walk the three flights down to her car. As her heels clicked rhythmically on the marble steps of the modern skyscraper, the weariness and depression hit her suddenly like a tidal wave. It was always the same, she thought. Everyone functioned at fever pitch to see the job through, working early and late, weekends when necessary, to meet the deadline. When suddenly it was all over came the depression, the exhaustion, the nosedive into a black vacuum, a void where even eating and sleeping became too much of an effort. They all knew it would happen, and yet they still overwound, dragging from their reserves the energy and freshness to stay in top gear in spite of desperate tiredness.

And yet it was her life and she loved it. She had been with the Foster Patterson Advertising Agency for nearly two years and Jake Humphries' personal assistant for almost half that time. Jake Humphries was not only the senior accounts director at the agency, but was heading for the post of managing director whenever Mark Foster decided to retire. All the most important accounts were handled by Jake Humphries and his team of accounts managers and executives.

That afternoon the weeks of hard effort had suddenly seemed well worthwhile when Davina checked the boardroom, ready and waiting for the presentation. The shining, polished mahogany table flanked by leather upholstered chairs gleamed in the sunlight on the seventh floor. A copy of the campaign schedule prepared by Jake lay neatly at each place. Round the walls on baize-covered pin-boards ranged the charts, the layouts and sketches showing packaging ideas, colours, slogans and lettering examples. Mock-ups of artwork for magazine advertisements were pinned side by side with story-boards for television commercials and more sketches illustrating audience targets.

Presenting an advertising campaign for a new product was never easy. The client was well aware that the agency badly wanted the account and arrived waiting to be persuaded. The sessions had gone without a hitch. Jake was fluent and never once consulted his notes, working entirely from memory. He introduced his report, summarising, indicating how the agency would build the image for the product, calling on the media director and the creative director to enlarge on their own areas of work, and ended with his analysis of the costs involved.

Two hours later the client had gone, impressed with the quality of the work, complimenting Jake, and sending thanks to all concerned. But there had been no hint of a decision, and none was expected at this stage. Everyone was aware that other agencies were bidding for the account. Although a new teenage perfume was not a major product, it was important for Fosters to get it, to feel the client had the confidence in Jake and the agency to entrust them with a new product.

That evening there would be a discreet dinner with Mark Foster and his wife dining the chairman of the company. Jake would be there with one of his lovelies, Davina mused, grinning slightly. She wondered if it would be the beautiful, dark-haired and dark-eyed Andrea Temple. She was the current steady, and there were bets going in the agency that, because she had lasted longer than any of her predecessors, she might just get Jake Humphries to the altar.

On the ground floor Davina smiled briefly at the night porter just coming on duty in his glass cubicle. Leaving the chrome tower with its blind, tinted windows, she stepped into a warm and balmy evening, the dusk darkening round her as she made her way to the car park.

As she unlocked her black baby Fiat, her tired eyes were dazzled for a moment as the lights sprang up in the building she had just left. Floor by floor came to life as the cleaners took over the empty offices. She backed out of the car park, heading for North London and home just as the Foster Patterson Advertising came to ghostly life in large blue neon lettering above the main swing doors.

The car felt good, and she reflected again how lucky she was—a job she liked, her own flat and the car, nice clothes and even a gold watch to which she had treated herself on her last birthday. Not many girls of her age in London had it so good.

And yet she had worked for it. When she first came to London, drained and miserable, a scraggy nineteen-year-old, in a strange town and cut off from everything loved and familiar, she had nothing except a tentative booking at a youth hostel and a good reference for her typing and shorthand skills. But she had been determined not to feel sorry for herself. Early the first morning she had bought the likely-looking papers and marked up the employment agencies. By lunchtime she had a temporary job, and she continued temping for the following six weeks. Several of the firms where she worked had offered her permanent employment, but she had continued to trudge round different offices getting—as she later realised—valuable experience of business and people.

After a week she had moved to a basement bedsitter in Victoria, but found the area depressing with little green to enjoy at weekends. When she finally accepted a job in the small typing pool at Foster Patterson, working for Shirley Harris, the pool supervisor, she began to look for more permanent accommodation. This took time because she was adamant about not sharing. She valued her privacy above all things, and saved hard to put together a month's rent in advance and a deposit on a flat.

As soon as she saw the two large, light and airy rooms with balcony at the top of Mrs Blunt's house in Hampstead she had decided. The shared bathroom brought the rent just within her means and she had moved in the following week. Gradually she had added her own possessions, hunting in markets, jumble sales and second-hand shops for rugs, pictures, vases and odd glasses and bits of pottery, until she felt the flat was really hers and looked forward to coming home in the evenings. It did not take long after that to put down roots, in Hampstead where she was happy to shop and wander at weekends and at the agency where she was popular with the girls because she was not pushy and never applied for secretarial jobs when they were offered.

As she filled out and her looks improved there was no shortage of invitations from the smooth young executives in the offices. Some she accepted and others she politely declined. But she was never involved. When any of them demanded more than she was prepared to give, she would stop seeing them, and some wondered at the guarded look in her eyes even when she was laughing and gay. One or two resented this reserve, and one, David Hallam, had become serious rather quickly and had tried to delve into her past. Her last evening with him had not been pleasant. When she had refused to be drawn and retreated from him, he had accused her of being frigid, a prude and, worse, a tease. Davina did not respond to the insults, but she had been upset. She had managed to control her feelings until he had driven her home when he tried more than a tentative pass in his car. Dishevelled and more than a little overwrought, she had fled up the stairs, crying heavily, and subsided only after reaching the sanctuary of her flat, where she locked herself in. Since David she had not gone out with anyone else.

And then suddenly the even tenor of her life had changed. It began one Friday morning when she came in to work and Shirley Harris had caught her.

'Oh, Davina, I'm glad you're early, dear. Don't take off your coat. You're working upstairs today for Georgina

Ward. Let me see,' she consulted a file in her hand, 'that's room 501. You're to fill in for the secretary who's ill, so you might be up there for several days.'

Davina blinked nervously.

'Shirley, does it have to be me? I'd really rather stay here,' she said anxiously.

'Yes, dear, it has to be you. You're my best typist and that's what I was asked to supply. So off you go!' She looked at Davina, who still hadn't moved. 'There's no need to be nervous,' she smiled reassuringly. 'No one's going to eat you. You'll only be doing exactly what you do down here, that's all. And I believe Georgina is very nice to work for.'

The fifth floor, Davina knew, was reserved for the high-powered in the agency, and room 501 when she got to it proclaimed in large letters the words 'Jake Humphries'. She knocked and walked in when the pleasant 'Come in' sounded through the door.

There were two desks in the room, which was sunny and restfully decorated in soft brown and beige tones with fitted carpet, stylish modern coat rack, filing cabinets to tone with the walls and, in one corner, a tiny kitchenette behind louvred doors.

Georgina Ward, Davina guessed, was about thirty, tall, elegantly dressed in a smoky grey flannel suit with white silk shirt. Her short curly blonde hair was stylishly cut, and her make-up was impeccable. Blue eyes regarded Davina steadily for a moment as she stood hesitating in the doorway.

'You must be Davina Richards,' she said, unwinding long, silk-clad legs and walking towards Davina with out-stretched hand. 'Do come and sit down . . . here, let me take your coat.' She hung up Davina's coat and gestured to a chair by her desk.

'I wish we could have a chat, but we're so frantic at the moment there's not the time. I'm hoping I can just throw you in at the deep end and let you get on with it. If you're with us a little while you'll soon pick up the gist of things, and perhaps there'll be more time to talk in a day or so.'

The bell buzzed on her desk and she flicked the intercom. A deep masculine voice sounded impatiently.

'Has that wretched girl turned up yet, Georgie?'

Davina flushed a deep crimson with embarrassment, and Georgina winked at her.

'Yes, Jake, just arrived.'

'At last!' the voice continued smoothly. 'Settle her quickly and come in, there's a good girl.' The intercom clicked off.

'Right.' Georgina picked up a file from her desk. 'This is the most urgent job. The script has to be typed and finished today. Here's the original, and I've sorted out a sample to show you how to set it out.'

Davina murmured that she had done scripts before.

'That's great, because you won't be seeing much of me today. There's paper and everything you'll need in your desk. I've emptied the bottom drawer for your personal things, and you can help yourself to coffee. Only make sure there's always fresh for the boss. If the phone rings when I'm not here, just take a message and leave it for me. Your lunch hour today you can just take when you want. Any questions?'

'No, thank you,' Davina said politely.

'Good. I'll leave you to it. I hope you enjoy your time with us,' said Georgina with a smile, and, picking up files, notebook and pencils, she disappeared through the inner door behind her desk.

Umpteen cups of coffee and weary hours later Davina looked up from the final checking of the finished script. The time on the wall clock was seven-fifteen. She heaved a sigh of relief and stacked the script carefully on Georgina's desk. There had been no one in the office since four o'clock, and she left all the messages laid out before she picked up her coat and, with a last glance round the room, switched off the lights and opened the door.

The inner office door opened suddenly, and she turned to see a man silhouetted in the doorway, the light from a desk lamp behind him, his face in darkness.

'Who the hell are you?' his irate voice demanded.

'I'm Davina Richards,' she answered quietly, 'and I've been working for Georgina today . . . there's no need to swear,' she finished coolly, and made to leave.

'Just a moment!' The clipped tones were a command. He came into the office and switched on the lights, and Davina had her first look at Jake Humphries.

He was big—there was no other way to describe him. He was not just tall, but broad-shouldered, deep-chested and long-legged. He had discarded his coat and tie, but even in shirt sleeves and hip-hugging smooth trousers it was obvious he was a powerful man. His face was deeply tanned with a jutting and clefted chin above which a sculpted, wide mouth now moved into a slightly mocking smile. A strong aquiline nose below dark straight eyebrows which were drawn into a slight frown and set above deep grey eyes almost the same colour as her own, Davina noted absently. Thick, jet black hair with some flecks of grey swept back from the wide forehead and curled slightly into the collar.

He was a man with endless self-confidence and totally male. And also, she judged, a man with no need whatever to prove his masculinity to anyone. It was so strongly virile, it was almost tangible, and she withdrew slightly from it.

As she was studying him she became aware of his gaze. He looked her over from the top of her auburn hair, heavily coiled into her neck, down her slender figure and long legs, his eyes returning to her face and the wide grey eyes, the tiptilted nose and creamy skin. His look lingered on the soft curve of her mouth, so that Davina coloured slightly and put her firm chin up at him.

'I apologise,' he drawled. 'I had no idea there was anyone still here. You've been very quiet. Why didn't I hear the typewriter?'

'I finished typing some time ago. For the last two hours I've been checking the script.'

'Are you from the typing pool?' he demanded suddenly.

She nodded.

'Right,' he said dismissively, I'll see you Monday.'

He turned away and with a crisp 'Goodnight' he went back into his office and closed the door.

After that day events moved swiftly. Georgina's secretary never reappeared and Davina found herself working so hard she had no time to worry about returning to the typing pool. Within a month she had became a permanent member of the Humphries team. She met Mike Davies, the shy, slim accounts manager, with a shock of blond hair and a soft voice. She liked him on sight and was soon invited to his home to meet his petite dark wife, Susan, and their two small black-eyed daughters, for whom she would baby-sit to give Mike and Susan a chance to go out in the evenings. Charlie Clarke was the young trainee accounts executive of the group, wild-eyed, red-haired and a real wolf. He was witty and very bright with an assured future in advertising ahead of him and an ambition to match his talents. Then there was Georgina and her husband Larry, himself in advertising with a media consultancy. They became very special friends in those early months and took Davina about with them in the advertising world. Larry was a good deal older than his wife with an unhappy marriage and divorce behind him, and he adored and cosseted Georgina with every look and gesture.

After a time Davina invited them up for the odd scratch meal, until her dinners became a regular part of the team's social life and her cooking an endless topic for banter and chat.

And at work there was Jake Humphries himself, demanding from all of them their very best, refusing to tolerate anything less. His standards were high, and anyone who fell below them was somehow no longer on the team, finding themselves with other groups, transferred to different jobs. Members of the team were envied and resented by many in the agency, but there were some who sighed with relief that they had more tolerant and less demanding bosses.

Davina's own initiation ceremony came about six weeks after she joined them. One morning she was told she would accompany Jake on a presentation in Georgina's stead. They went into his office for the briefing, and she was exposed to one of his famous scrutinies.

'All right,' he said briskly, 'turn around.'

She had done so, feeling exceedingly foolish.

'No, not like that!' he said sharply. 'Slowly.'

She tried again.

'Take it easy, Jake, 'Georgina pointed out, 'this is all new to Davina.'

'What?' he looked at Georgina, his mind obviously elsewhere, 'what do you mean? Oh, yes, I see.' He turned impatiently back to Davina. 'I don't really know where to start.' He came up to her, standing close. 'Your hair——' he went on slowly, and reached out to touch it with his fingers. She flinched away, but he didn't seem to notice, engrossed in his own thoughts.

'Mm, don't have it cut,' he said next, 'but try and have it done differently, not so severe and tightly back from the face.'

'Why don't I take her to Antoine?' Georgina suggested. 'He'll know what to do about it.

'What a good idea.' Jake was relieved. 'Now,' he went on with his impersonal inspection, 'it isn't any one thing. It's the way you think about yourself ... the walk, the carriage.' He paused for a moment. 'You know, you're a beautiful girl,' he said in surprise, 'but you don't look as though you know it.' He stepped back. 'And you must get rid of those clothes,' he ended.

Davina's face went a bright red. 'I don't think all this is necessary just for one occasion,' she said acidly.

'Mm . . .?' he queried, and looked into her face, noting her heightened colour. For a moment, grey eyes met grey and Davina felt a strange electric tension crackle between them. Then his eyes were veiled, his head thrown back in a familiar posture and she looked away.

Georgina spoke crisply. 'I think we know what you have

in mind. We'll take a couple of hours over lunch and deal
with it.'

'Yes, do,' Jake's voice was withdrawn. 'Oh, and
Georgina,' he turned to her, suddenly alert and businesslike, 'this is all on expenses.'

'No!' Davina's voice was loud. 'No, thank you,' she
said more quietly. 'I couldn't ... I wouldn't want to
accept that.'

Georgina intervened quickly.

'Don't worry about it, Davina. We'll settle all that
later,' and she went out.

Jake was leaning casually against the corner of his big
desk, and Davina looked up to find his gaze on her, his
eyes narrowed in concentration. He seemed about to say
something more, but she turned abruptly and walked out
on rather unsteady legs.

Later that morning she watched her own transforma-
tion in an endless series of mirrors. Antoine cut and dried,
draped and pinned her hair, showing how she could now
wear it loose if she wished, advising her how to soften the
outline with deep waves either side of her head. While
he was working and talking to her persuasively, the mani-
curist shaped her nails, finishing with a pale pink
natural varnish that gave her hands a glamorous, femin-
ine look.

At the exclusive salon where Georgina took her next,
she tried on one outfit after another, and finally settled on
an oatmeal Chanel suit with flattering nipped-in waistline,
turn-back cuffs and soft satin shirt in tobacco brown with
matching kid leather pumps and sheer silk tights.

Finally, at the beauty salon in Bond Street, she had a
massage, facial and a session with the make-up expert,
who explained to her how the planes of her face, the high
cheekbones and wide-set eyes needed only the softest
shades of subtle lip-gloss, eye-shadow and foundation.
When she was finished and Georgina paraded her before
a full-length mirror, Davina could only gaze speechless at
the stranger reflected in the glass.

That was a day she would never forget, because it saw

the death of the scraggy miserable teenager, and her new poise and self-confidence stemmed from the moment she looked at herself in that mirror.

It was some months later when she was summoned one morning to Jake's office. He wanted to see her alone. She quaked in her shoes, knowing there was only one reason for an interview alone with the boss, and that was a transfer. She had done something unforgivable, committed some awful blunder, and she would be transferred or fired. She remembered vividly her clammy hands and the nervous constriction in her throat, as she told herself it didn't matter. There were other jobs, this was not the only one in town.

In his office she sat nervously, her hands clasped in her lap, looking up at him from the other side of his desk. And he had told her quietly and quite impersonally that Georgina was leaving to have a baby, and he wanted her, Davina, to take over Georgina's job.

At first she thought it was a joke. Then she had been more petrified than she had ever felt before. And finally she had taken it in and had accepted.

Jake explained it all very carefully and coolly. He thought quite certainly she was ready to take it on. All she lacked was self-confidence, and this she should get from Georgina in the following two months during her training.

It had all sounded so simple when he talked about it, but Davina knew from experience that things always sounded easy when Jake described them. But there had been help and encouragement from the rest of the team, who showed their approval, taking her out to celebrate. Later that evening Larry told her Georgina was delighted since it had been her idea in the first place.

And it had worked out. Davina had been doing the job for nearly a year and she still loved it.

She saw the envelope on the hall table as soon as she opened the front door. There had been no warning the day would end like this, she thought. She had not seen that writing for nearly two years, but she knew it instantly.

Upstairs she put it on one side, refused to open it, dreading the moment when she would have to read it.

A bath first, she decided, something to eat. Then she would be in a better frame of mind for whatever it contained.

An hour later she sat with the letter in her lap, an untasted sandwich on the table in front of her.

'Mr and Mrs David Richards request the pleasure of your company on the occasion of the wedding of their daughter, Monica Anne. . . .' The heavily embossed invitation stared at her. Next Saturday—a week away. Mechanically she got up, standing the invitation on the mantelpiece. It was then she saw the postscript on the back in her mother's writing.

'Please come, darling. We all want you here.' The 'all' was heavily underlined.

Davina bent her head to lean against the fireplace and started to cry.

CHAPTER TWO

JAKE HUMPHRIES was early the following Monday morning. Davina was just putting on the Cona for coffee when he arrived and swept through into his own office with a brief, 'You're early, Davina.'

Before he could settle she followed him, closing the door behind her, and he looked up in surprise. She didn't usually come in till he had gone through his letters.

'Could I speak to you for a moment?' she said, her voice empty of expression.

'Yes, of course,' he replied, noting the deep shadows under her eyes and the pallor of her face. He gestured to her to sit down, but she shook her head.

'This will only take a moment.' She swallowed. 'Could I take next Friday off, please?'

'Yes, of course,' he said without hesitation, and then, sharply, 'There's nothing wrong, is there?'

She looked down at her hands and found she was clenching them tightly.

'No, of course not,' she said quickly, and turned to go.

'Davina!' he said again sharply, and she stopped. 'Er . . . I believe you still have some leave to come. If you want to take a few days, please do. We're bound to have a fairly quiet week. In fact I shall be going away myself before the week-end.'

'Thank you,' she said, 'but no. Just the one day on Friday. I'll make sure Heather can cope.'

She looked at him guardedly, controlling her voice with care. She must not start crying again.

'Very well,' he said at last, looking at her rather searchingly, but she refused to meet his eyes.

'Thank you,' she said again, and walked out on rather wobbly legs. Sinking into her own chair, she suddenly realised it was going to be a difficult week. Perhaps she should have agreed to take the whole week. But that would have left her at home with nothing to do but think, the last thing she wanted.

'Good morning!' Heather's cheerful voice and sturdy presence interrupted Davina's thoughts as her secretary walked in, young, tomboyish, her brown curly hair flying round the fresh face. She was a tonic and had a cheerful line in chatter which kept them all laughing when things were tense.

'Hello, Heather,' Davina greeted her. 'The coffee's ready, I think. Would you please take it in?'

'Sure thing,' and Heather flung off her coat.

The week was under way and it turned out to be one of the worst Davina could remember. Not a day passed without mistakes, and they were all hers—messages she forgot, meetings she failed to remind Jake about, and even a telephone call from Andrea Temple she cut off by mistake.

At that point Jake lost his cool, and stormed into her office.

'Davina, what the hell happened this time?' he shouted. 'Have you cut me off? For heaven's sake pull yourself together and start thinking, girl. We can't go on like this!'

'I'm sorry,' she said quietly, and began to dial the number of Miss Temple's flat.

'Never mind,' he said more quietly. 'Just give me a line and I'll dial it myself.' He went back into his own room, and Davina found she was trembling so badly she had to sit down.

Heather looked at her in concern.

'Here,' Davina found her suddenly at her side with a cup of coffee, 'you'd better try this. I wish I had something stronger.' And she went back to her desk. 'It's none of my business, Davina,' she began heatedly, 'but. . . .'

'Leave it,' Davina interrupted harshly, 'just let it be. And you're right, it is none of your business.' She gathered up her things and put on her jacket. 'I'm going for an early lunch,' she said shortly. 'Will you please take messages and stay until I come back. Then you can go for yours.'

'Yes, of course, Davina,' said Heather, rather chastened.

Davina picked up a taxi and asked to be dropped at the entrance to Hyde Park. It was a cool, crisp morning, the huge chestnuts ready to burst into blossom overhead and the multi-coloured crocuses adding their own colourful pattern to the carpet of green grass underfoot. She walked heedless of early morning couples and the tramps emerging from their newspapers.

'I can't go on like this,' she thought listlessly. 'If I'm not careful I'll lose my job.'

Perhaps it had been a mistake to accept the invitation. And yet she had felt confident she could cope, she could face them all. And she would have to go back some time; she owed that to her parents.

An hour later she returned to the office feeling much better, resolved to put all thoughts of the week-end away and concentrate on the work in hand. The rest of the day passed without mishaps.

She was packing on Thursday evening when the phone rang on the landing below. She heard voices and then Mrs Blunt calling.

'Miss Richards, telephone for you!'

She opened her door. 'Thank you . . . just coming.'

She hurried downstairs. 'Hello,' she said, slightly breathless.

'Davina?' It was Jake Humphries' voice.

She swallowed convulsively. What had she done this time? For him to call her at home meant it was something serious.

'Davina, is that you?' His voice sounded impatient.

'Yes.' Her voice was high-pitched with nervousness. 'What's happened? What's gone wrong now?'

There was a pause while she realised what she had said. 'Oh, dear,' she thought

'Yes . . . well. . . .' Amusement sounded in Jake's voice for the first time that week, 'it's me this time. I've left the new crisps contract in the office, and I need it to study

over the week-end. I wondered if you could pick it up
and bring it to me here.'

There was a silence while he waited for her to say
something.

'Are you there, Davina?' he said at last. 'Can you hear
me?'

'Yes,' she found her voice again, 'certainly.'

'You mean you can do it? You see,' he explained, 'I
have to wait for this call from the States and I don't want
to leave, but if you can't get away I could try and get to
the office in the morning before I leave London.'

'No,' she said quickly, 'that's all right. I'll get it.'

'Good girl,' he said briskly. 'I'll get a mini-cab to pick
you up in half an hour.' He hung up.

The night porter knew her and unlocked the offices.
Within an hour of the telephone call she was at Jake
Humphries' front door.

The flat was on the top floor of a prestigious block in
Knightsbridge overlooking the park. Davina had been
there before, once at a party he had given to the office
staff when he was made a board director, and once when
he was ill and she had come to take dictation.

He opened the door himself, wearing tight black cords
and a black cashmere sweater. The casual clothes emphasised his height and the darkness of his hair. He looked
somehow quite lethal in the casual clothes and Davina
felt vaguely ill at ease as they looked at each other for a
moment.

'Thank you,' he said, and reached out his hand. She
put the file into it and turned to go, but he moved forward
and gripped her arm, moving her gently past him into
the flat.

She remembered the tiled hall with the boating prints
round the walls, and stood awkwardly waiting to know
what he wanted of her. She was anxious to be gone.

He smiled. 'You will stay and have a drink, won't
you?'

'No, thank you ... I ... have to get back,' she stammered slightly. 'I'm packing.'

'So am I,' he said, 'and I do dislike it, but Mrs Webber, my housekeeper, is on holiday and so I'm lumbered. Please come in a moment while I just check this.' And he ushered her into the living room.

The room looked exactly the same. Large and high-ceilinged, it was restful though very masculine, with books lining two of the walls, hi-fi equipment and television built into shelves on the third and the forth wall a huge glass window with doors leading out on to the wide balcony. The deep-pile brown carpet went from wall to wall and two enormous leather sofas faced the fireplace where a small grate held a large log giving off a cosy warmth against the chill of the evening.

Jake turned to her. 'You will have a small drink, won't you? To keep me company?' He turned towards her and she noticed how lightly he moved for such a big man, something she would not see in the office where he rarely removed the jacket or waistcoat of his impeccably tailored suits.

'Can't I persuade you?' he coaxed, and she was suddenly aware of his charm. She had so often observed it at work when he turned it on to clinch a deal or persuade a client. But it had never been directed at her before, and she could sympathise with the Andrea Temples in this world because they never seemed to leave him. It was always he who moved on.

She must be feeling rather weak and lightheaded to think like this, she thought. It seemed suddenly churlish to refuse.

'A small dry sherry, please,' she said, and smiled serenely up at him, unaware of the glow that radiated from her eyes across her face.

Jake stood quite still for a moment, looking down at her, the smile gone from his eyes, a fleeting look of surprise flickering across his expression. Then it was gone and he moved over to the drinks cabinet.

'I hope you're planning a pleasant week-end,' he said conversationally. 'I'm off to the parental home to see my father who's not been too well lately.'

'Oh, I'm sorry. Nothing serious, I hope?'

She took her glass from him and they both sat down, Jake stretching his long legs to the fire.

'He does too much when I'm not there. I go down as often as I can and read him the riot act, which he enjoys.' He grinned rather boyishly over at her. 'But what about you?' he asked insistently.

Davina realised he was going to persevere and decided it was time to leave.

'Yes, I'm going away for the week-end too,' she said, determined not to be drawn.

'Going home?' he asked quietly.

'Yes,' she said shortly, and got up.

'Another drink?' His voice was merely polite.

'No, thank you. I must be off . . . can I get a taxi?'

'Of course. I'll get you one.'

He got up and moved over to her, standing so close she could smell the aftershave he used. She was tall herself, but felt dwarfed by his height and his nearness. She had to force herself to stand still, not to back away as she would have liked.

'Davina, what is it?' He had his coaxing voice on again. 'Can't you tell me? We've all been aware this week that something is troubling you and we've all been concerned. Perhaps I might be able to help if you could tell me.'

This time she did back away in panic, turning her back on him, forcing the tears back from beneath her eyelids.

'I know I've been inefficient this week, and I'm sorry,' she bit her lip, trying to keep her voice steady, 'but you needn't worry about that any more. It's all being sorted out. I shall be quite all right when I get back next week. I just haven't been very well.' She knew she was babbling and stopped.

'I see.' His voice was immediately behind her and she moved away from him so abruptly she knocked into a coffee table, hitting her leg just below the knee. She toppled forward with a cry of pain as he caught her from behind, breaking her fall and turning her round into his arms.

She was so surprised she didn't move, and Jake kept his arms round her lightly. Putting up one hand to her hair, he pushed her head down gently against his chest. There was nothing intimate or frightening in his hold, although she could feel her heart hammering. She stayed quite still in his embrace as he began to massage the back of her neck, easing the pain she had had all week.

'You've had a headache, haven't you,' he murmured quietly.

Weakly she let him, feeling the comfort of his broadness, strangely at peace and secure in his arms. He didn't say anything more and she began to relax in his hold. His hands were warm and strong against her neck and shoulders as he massaged away the taut knotted muscles, his touch impersonal and expert. Eventually she stirred and he put her away from him gently, sitting her down in the corner of one of the sofas.

'Just don't move,' he said lightly, not looking at her. 'I'm going to get some food and coffee.' Davina looked up at him to protest, but he forestalled her. 'I haven't eaten either, and Mrs Webber will have left something simmering. Just stay there and rest for a moment.'

She leaned her head back, letting the warmth of the fire lull her into a light doze. She opened her eyes to find Jake had drawn up a low trolley on which plates were warming and food was keeping hot. A delicious smell reached her, and she sat up with a guilty start.

Two large china table lamps had been switched on to cast a soft light over carpet, books and walls. Jake was standing with his back to her looking out at the darkening skyline.

'Oh, dear, I must have dropped off!' She spoke hesitantly. 'I'm sorry, You should have woken me.'

'There was no hurry.' He turned towards her and she thought his face looked taut and rather grim in the lamplight. She wondered if he was angry she was still here, or bored. 'It was probably the warmth from the fire,' he went on coldly. 'I often find myself dropping off sitting

here in the evenings.' He came and sat down opposite
her. 'I've kept everything hot and I hope you don't mind
eating here informally rather than the dining room.' He
leaned over to the food. 'Now let me help you to some of
this.'

'Thank you,' she said shyly. 'Could I please have a
quick wash?'

'Of course,' he got up, 'how remiss of me. It's through
here.'

He went ahead of her through the hall and down a
long corridor at the end of which he opened the door to a
bathroom. It was in pale green with tiles and toning
carpet, matching towels and huge glass-stoppered jars
holding body lotions, perfumed cottonwool pads, bath oil
and talcum powders. All mod. cons. for the visiting
female, Davina noted drily.

Appalled at the sight of herself in the long mirror, she
washed, brushed out her hair and re-knotted it softly. A
touch of lipstick and she was ready.

They ate in silence that was strangely companionable,
and Davina appreciated the quiet, feeling no need to talk.
Over coffee Jake talked to her lightly of work and of his
boat. Sailing, she learnt, was his hobby, and he had a
sailing boat at his father's house. She was content to listen,
watching the firelight playing over the room.

'Goodness!' she exclaimed suddenly, catching sight of
the time. 'I hadn't realised how late it is. I really must go.'

'Of course you must,' Jake said lightly, 'and we both
have to finish packing. But I'm still serious about listening
to you, helping if I can. Sometimes just talking about
something helps.'

She thought about it for a moment. His interest was
no idle curiosity, nor was it personal. He was concerned
with her work, her efficiency. Did she owe it to him to tell
him? Did she want to tell him, to talk to him? Could she
talk about it at all?

'I'm a good listener,' he added.

Davina didn't respond.

'You know don't you that you can trust me. I hope I

don't have to tell you that anything said here tonight is strictly confidential and will go no farther.'

She blushed furiously. He must have read her mind. She was concerned about her colleagues, chatting perhaps behind her back. She looked across at him to find his eyes intently on her.

'I . . . it's late,' she said lamely.

'Yes,' he said firmly, 'it is. But it's also important, Davina. I'm not pushing you to talk to me. But if you want to talk about it, I'm here.'

She started to speak, slowly and haltingly.

'I'm going home this week-end . . . for my sister's wedding, and it will be the first time I've been home since I left two years ago.'

She glanced across at him, but he was gazing into the fire with no sign of emotion in his face.

'My parents' home is in a small village where all the families know each other. This is very nice in some ways, but it can be difficult in times of crisis. When I left, my family were in such a crisis. The whole village knew about it and . . . I was the cause.

'My sister is five years older than I am and we've always been very close. She went to university in Edinburgh to study, because she's very bright. I've always been the quiet one of the family, and I'm not ambitious. When she was in her last year at Edinburgh I left school and took a shorthand and typing course. Then I got a job locally at the local dairy depot. When I'd been there about three months I was told I would be transferred to a new marketing manager who was coming down from London.

'That's how I met Philip. He rented a cottage outside the village and soon we were . . . I . . . well, we started going out together, and. . . .' She stopped, her mouth suddenly dry, clutched by the fear that always overcame her when she remembered.

'He fell in love with you,' Jake finished for her, remote and impersonal.

'Yes . . . well, I discovered that later . . . at first I just knew I . . . how I felt.'

She breathed in deeply, trying to clear the constriction in her throat.

'He was marvellous, everything I always dreamed a man could be ... handsome, sophisticated, experienced, and ... I was very happy. My parents weren't pleased, they thought he was too old for me ... he was quite a bit older. But we became engaged and then the wedding date was fixed. I felt I was the luckiest girl in the world. My parents were determined to give me a big wedding, no expense spared, and my mother ...' she choked a little, 'she ordered everything—flowers, caterers, the hotel reception, bridesmaids, and they dug into their savings quite a bit. Then Philip and I had a sort of ... er ... disagreement. I was very young and had strong ideas about some things. ...'

'Darling,' Philip had said casually one Sunday, 'I have to go on a trip north to the Scottish office. How about coming with me?'

'How long will you be away?' she hesitated.

'Oh, only a few days, perhaps a week.'

Davina had considered.

'I'd have to take the time off my holiday leave and it would mean cutting short the honeymoon.'

'Well, just come for a few days, a long week-end. I do want you with me,' he coaxed, and agreed she would go with him.

Arrived at the pleasant, friendly family hotel in Edinburgh, Davina was at first not aware Philip had signed them in as husband and wife. When the porter addressed her as Mrs Andrews, she dismissed it as a natural mistake.

It was when she saw the room with its huge fourposter bed where the porter put both their cases that she began to feel uneasy. Left alone, she tried the second door, hoping to find another bedroom, but it was a bathroom.

When Philip came up she made light of it.

'They've given us a double instead of two singles, darling, by mistake.'

'No mistake, my sweet,' he said gently, taking her in his arms. 'I think it's about time we really got to know each other, don't you? I've waited patiently because you're so young, but you know how much I love you. We're going to get married, and there's no need to wait any longer. In fact, I think it's important we discover each other before any vows are made at the altar, don't you?'

He kissed her lovingly, his lips lingering against her mouth. But her response was not there.

'No, Philip,' she said tremulously. 'I do want to wait until we're married.'

He didn't say anything. Instead he pulled her tightly into his arms and kissed her passionately, taking her lips hard with his, running his hands possessively down her back as he pressed his body into her soft curves. She felt confused and did not resist.

'You know I adore you,' he said hoarsely. 'I won't hurt you. You needn't be afraid. Just don't think about it, and give yourself to me.' He bent to kiss her throat lightly and began to undo her blouse, pushing his mouth lower down to touch her breast.

And then Davina knew she didn't want this. She was not exactly sure why, but she slipped out of his arms and stood facing him.

'No, Philip, this isn't the way I want it—like a dress rehearsal with an option to call off the first night. It's not like that for me. I love you, I want to marry you and . . . I want you,' she ended shyly.

'Of course, darling,' he coaxed her, 'I feel the same. But I'm a man, and I've been faithful to you almost from the beginning. You must understand I've been very patient. If you love me, you'll give me now what I want and what I need. I thought you understood that when you agreed to come up here with me.'

He paused for a moment, his eyes on the shadow between her breasts where he had unbuttoned her blouse.

'You know how desirable you are and you know how passionately I feel about you. I thought you felt the same.'

She turned away, trying to think clearly. Why did she feel this surge of disappointment? Was she being foolishly romantic, unrealistic and even selfish? She knew most girls she met would not hesitate, would in fact have made love with their fiancé long before this. Why did she have this revulsion at the idea of anticipating their wedding? Before she could reply Philip spoke lightly.

'I tell you what, darling—I'll leave you now for a while. Have a rest, order yourself some tea and then get ready for me to take you out. We'll go somewhere romantic tonight and drink wine and look into each others' eyes. By that time you might feel ready for what we both want. We do both want it?' he insisted.

Davina swallowed nervously and nodded rather unhappily.

'All right, I'll have a rest,' she whispered.

'I'll see you tonight, then,' he said coolly, 'and do stop worrying. If you really don't want it, I won't force you in any way. I'll simply get myself another room.'

At that she spun round into his arms.

'Oh, darling, I knew you'd understand!' she laughed with relief.

Philip stepped back from her, surprise on his face. Then he kissed her briefly and left.

She had come back from Edinburgh two days later, vaguely worried by their time together. Philip had been kind and loving as always, but somehow different. He had seemed unreachable and refused to talk seriously about anything. He had made one more attempt to get her to change her mind, to persuade her to share his room, but she had been adamant.

'Davina!' it was Jake's voice. 'Are you all right?'

'Oh, I'm sorry.' She blushed fiercely.

'You were away in dreamland.'

'Yes . . . well, you see, Philip and I went away on a trip together,' she went on carefully, 'and we didn't see eye to eye about . . . being together, so I came home again.'

That sounded rather lame and she had no idea if Jake understood what she was trying to say. But he didn't speak and didn't look at her. He leaned forward and put another log on the fire, his face impassive.

'Anyway, when we got back, I found that ... I discovered that. ...' Her voice shook.

'Take your time,' Jake said quietly.

She leaned back in the sofa and tried to relax, remembering. ...

Philip had not come back until the following Friday. She had missed him and wondered again if she had acted unwisely. Perhaps she had been wrong in her attitude; she knew some of her girl friends thought her a prude. But as soon as he walked into the office all her fears were swept away. He was loving as always, if not more so, and they arranged to meet that night.

Coming home from work she had been surprised to see her sister Monica, who had appeared for the weekend, an extravagance she explained by saying she had suddenly felt lonely for the family. She seemed quiet and subdued, but Davina was too wrapped up in her own happiness and her plans for the evening to pay much attention to several lengthy telephone calls her sister made.

She had had a lovely evening with Philip at the local steak house, talking about Christmas with his sister and her family and their January wedding. When they came back to the house she felt happy and at peace.

Monica was in one of her moods, and Davina noticed vaguely that she and Philip seemed to be at loggerheads, arguing and rowing over nothing. Monica seemed bent on picking a fight with him, until at last he was goaded into shouting at her.

'Why don't you go, then, if you can't be civil?'

Davina was amazed. She had never heard Philip shout, and was glad her parents were out for the evening.

'What's the matter with you two tonight?' she asked. 'You're both so bad-tempered, for no reason that I can see.'

'I'll be off,' Monica said curtly.

'Don't be silly,' Philip answered shortly, 'there isn't a

train north tonight. How would you get back?' And then, unexpectedly, 'I'll go and relieve you both of my company.'

'Oh, darling,' Davina said contritely, 'I didn't mean anything!'

But he wouldn't be deterred and he went. Davina saw him to the door and they bade each other a loving goodnight.

She was cheerful after he had gone and went to make some coffee. Bringing it into the living room, she saw her sister was still tense, and could get nothing out of her. Then Monica said suddenly, 'He's no good for you, you know.'

'What are you talking about?' Davina asked, her mind still with Philip.

'I'm talking about Philip,' Monica said angrily, 'your fiancé.'

'I don't know why you're so steamed up,' Davina countered. 'You've been strung up since you arrived. It's not like you. Anyway, lay off Philip. He's my fiancé and I love him. It doesn't concern you.' She realised she was speaking quite sharply.

'That's the trouble,' Monica said cryptically.

'I still don't know what this is all about. What have you suddenly against him? You always liked him before, and nothing's changed.'

'Well, if you must know, I went out with him in Edinburgh,' Monica blurted out.

'Oh, did you?' Davina asked. 'After I'd gone?'

'Yes.'

'Oh, well, that was nice of him.'

'Not particularly. He was lonely.'

'Well,' Davina said again, 'I'm sorry if you didn't get on, but that's not my fault.'

'We did get on,' Monica said quietly. 'Too well.'

There was a pause and Davina gave her sister her concentrated attention. The room seemed suddenly deadly quiet. Neither of the girls moved.

'Could you explain that?' Davina said eventually,

striving for composure.

'I don't think I have to, do I?' Monica said bitterly.
'You know me, don't you, from the old days? What do
you think happened?'

'You found yourselves ... attracted to each other. . . .'
Davina could feel the rise of hysteria in her throat.

'Yes.'

'I see,' she said, deadly calm. 'Then in future you won't
want to meet alone again.'

Monica said nothing.

'What happened?' Davina's voice was expressionless.

'Can't you imagine? Do I really have to spell it out?'
Monica's voice quivered.

'Yes, you do,' Davina said harshly, fighting for control.

'I can't,' Monica whispered.

'You kissed ... perhaps cuddled.' Davina's voice was
ice-cold.

'And some!' Monica spoke defiantly, not looking at her
younger sister. 'Oh, what's the use? You're going to find
out sooner or later. . . . We made love.'

'Not completely?' Davina begged.

'Yes, completely.'

'I don't believe you,' Davina said raggedly.

'You needn't.' For some reason Monica's voice was
bitter. 'But you've got your revenge already,' she stormed.
'He made love to me—yes, and not once, but every night,
all night. And what happened? I fell in love with him.
Isn't that hilarious? Doesn't it make you scream with
laughter? Me! The love 'em and leave 'em kid. And what
does he feel for me? Nothing. Nothing, do you hear me,
Davina? It's you he loves, you he adores. And he feels
nothing but guilt and fear in case you find out. That's all
he cares about. You know what he said afterwards? He
was tempted because I was so like you.'

The deathly quiet in the room was endless as Monica
stopped speaking. Davina's face was stony, her eyes deep
pools of shock and horror. It wasn't real and she didn't
believe yet. But, knowing her sister, she knew somewhere
it was all true. Philip. . . . Her body went rigid and her

hands broke the cup she was holding. The pieces scattered everywhere and the sudden noise released some kind of tension in Monica. She began to cry, softly at first, hopelessly and then uncontrollably, the sobs shaking her body, the tears streaming down her face.

At last Davina moved. Mechanically and almost without volition she got up, walked into the hall, picked her coat from the rack and opened the front door.

A sudden crack as a log fell into the hearth brought Davina back to her surroundings to find Jake looking at her rather blankly. She pulled herself together.

'It's difficult,' she said quietly. 'I'll try and make it brief.' She smiled lightly, but he saw the smile did not reach her eyes which held a strangely haunted look. He turned away to stoke the fire which now burned brightly, the flames leaping up the chimney and the brass fender reflecting the light into the room.

She spoke more firmly.

'I discovered that Philip and my sister met in Edinburgh after I left. They . . . liked each other and . . . they had a brief affair.'

For the first time Jake asked a question.

'How did you find that out?' His voice was harsh.

'I . . . my sister told me.' Davina paused, trying to find the right words. 'She fell in love with him, but he apparently did not love her. He still wanted to marry me. That's what Monica told me. I didn't see Philip again. I left the next day and haven't been back since.'

Jake didn't say anything. He waited, still looking intently into the fire, then he leaned forward and took a fresh cheroot and lit it slowly.

'At the time I was most concerned about my parents,' Davina went on. 'I didn't want them to find out what had happened. It was bad enough for them that I was pulling out of the wedding . . . the love and expense, the work my mother had put into it . . . it was a bad time.' She stopped for a moment to gain control over her voice. 'I told my parents we'd discovered we didn't suit after all. I thought my father would be pleased, but he wasn't. He didn't believe me. He knew how much I loved Philip, and he thought had Philip jilted me.'

She stopped to pull her thoughts together.

'Shortly afterwards Philip left the area and came back to London. Monica left university without finishing her degree course and went to live with him. My father never knew about that.'

Davina finished, dry-eyed, but drained of all emotion. The desire to cry had completely left her.

Eventually Jake spoke quietly, his voice flat and without expression. 'So who is your sister going to marry?'

'She's marrying Philip. It seems she's pregnant. My father doesn't know that . . . about her expecting a baby. He's not very well, and that's why my mother wants me to come to the wedding.' She swallowed. 'I think my mother feels if I'm there my father will finally accept that one of his daughters didn't cause the unhappiness of the other.' She went on slowly, 'I think the reason I've been so unhinged this week. . . .' she smiled faintly at that, 'is because I've been trying to find a way to convince him.'

Jake turned to look at her. 'And have you found a way?' he asked grimly.

'Yes, I think so.' She stopped and laughed, slightly embarrassed. 'So now you know it all.' She looked up at him. 'Thank you for listening. I think it's helped me to talk to someone. I never have, you see . . . talked about it, I mean.'

'Am I to be told how you propose to convince your father that you're happy without Philip?'

'Er . . . yes, if you're interested. It will sound a bit odd, but I couldn't think of anything better. . . .' She hesitated. 'I've . . . er . . . hired someone from an escort service to come with me and pretend to be my fiancé,' she finished rather quickly and breathlessly, flushing a deep red.

'I see.' Jake did not move. 'Is that why you're wearing a ring on your engagement finger this evening?'

'Oh, dear, I'd forgotten I'd put it on. I didn't remember to take it off before I came out . . . yes, that's why.' She stopped, knowing she was babbling again.

'Do you think it will?'

'Will . . .?' She looked at him questioningly.

'Do you think it will convince your father?'

'Oh, yes, I'm sure,' she said defensively.

'I see.'

Jake got up suddenly, walked to the window and then back again to look down at her.

'Why do you have to protect yourself in this way? Isn't there a boy-friend who could take care of you in a more . . . personal way?' His voice was oddly harsh.

She flushed again. 'No,' she said, raising her chin at him a little, facing the question in his eyes quite openly and honestly.

'That can only be because you don't wish for anyone. Many must have tried,' he said deliberately.

Davina didn't say anything to that, but her eyes dropped to her hands and she clenched one over the ring on the other.

Jake didn't move away. She wanted to get up, but couldn't do so without touching him.

'Do you still love him?' he asked harshly.

'Yes,' she admitted. 'That's why I can't go unprotected. I couldn't face it.'

Jake walked back to the window and she got up.

'Are you sure?'

'Oh, yes, I'm sure. I've tried to be with other people— I've wanted to be. But it doesn't work for me. I'm not proud of it, but I don't deny it. I've lived with it too long for that.' She turned to go. 'And now I really must go. Thank you again. Can I call a taxi?'

'Yes, in a moment.'

'No!' her voice was sharp and determined. 'No more, please. I don't want to talk any more.'

'I understand how tired you must be, but I want you to wait another moment.' His voice was determined and commanding with an undertone of something else she could not quite catch, almost an urgency.

'Where is your home, Davina? Which part of the

country?' he asked unexpectedly.

She looked at him in surprise.

'In Cornwall, near St Ives. Why?'

'Because I've a suggestion to make. Sit down again just for another minute.' He was using his coaxing voice again.

She sat down primly on a hard chair by the door.

He stood quite still, legs apart, facing her across the room, the light behind him as on that first day and she couldn't see his eyes.

'Davina, will you marry me?' he asked evenly.

CHAPTER THREE

DAVINA stared at him, quite unable to take in what he had just said, and for a moment there was complete silence in the room while neither moved. Then she spoke sharply, decisively.

'Of course I won't marry you! Is this some kind of joke?' She was angry now. 'If you're making fun of me, I'd like to remind you that it was you who wanted this talk, not I.'

Jake answered quietly, quite unmoved by her outburst.

'If you think I'd joke about what you've just told me, you know me even less than I think you do. It's a perfectly serious question, and I'll explain exactly what I have in mind.'

'I don't care what you have in mind! I'm leaving, and I'll find my own taxi!' She got up and moved to the door.

'Please, Davina,' he said coldly, 'sit down and stop babbling. I have something serious in mind of benefit to both of us, and I think you should give me the chance to explain it.'

'I've just told you I love another man and you propose marriage? And you think I'll benefit?' She was fast losing control, her voice rising.

'It's because you're in love with someone else, someone who's not free to love you, that I'm making this suggestion. Now are you going to listen?' She said nothing, and Jake went on more quietly, 'It may sound strange to you, but we're both in slightly similar positions.'

Her eyes flew to his face in shocked surprise. Surely he couldn't be in love with someone who wasn't free to marry him? She knew Andrea Temple was unmarried.

'You're in love with the man who's to be your sister's husband, and you need to convince your family that he's of no interest to you. For this you want a fiancé. I, too, need a fiancée, to convince my father that I'm preparing to settle down. Both situations require a temporary solution.'

He paused and sat down again, looking into the fire.

'I don't think you know much of my personal life.' He stated it as a fact and did not make it into a question. 'I'm an only child, and my family consists of my father who's a widower. His greatest wish is that I should be married and have children. Every time I go home I know he's hoping I'll bring someone who's to be my wife, so that he'll see a grandchild before he dies.'

His voice was low and Davina sensed he was finding it difficult to talk about his personal feelings for his father.

'He's not very well and may shortly have to face an operation. He is also not young—he was in his forties when I was born.'

Jake stopped and took a deep breath, then he turned in his chair to face her and she saw his face was strangely bleak.

'What I'm suggesting is this. When you need a fiancé to convince your family, I'll make myself available to you, and when I need a fiancée on visits to my father, you make yourself available to me.'

There was a stunned silence.

'But that's quite impossible ... it's dishonest,' she stammered. 'Your father ... he would expect you to marry, not just to be engaged, and. . . .'

'Let me finish, Davina,' he interrupted harshly. 'How long do you imagine it would take your father, who you say knows you well, to find out your escort for the day? Would it last out the week-end? And even if it did, what about the next time you visit them? Or they visit you in London? Would you try to find the same man again? What if he's not available, has left the escort service, doesn't want to come? How did you imagine all that would work out?'

'I've thought it out. Once the shock of meeting me again is over, I can ease them into the idea that I'm not the marrying kind, that I want a career and have no thought of marriage till I'm much older.'

Jake didn't say anything for a moment, and she felt she had convinced him. He sounded tired when he spoke again.

'And you really believe your father isn't going to guess? And be hurt even more deeply at your pretence? Do you want him to think you're so deeply hurt by Philip marrying your sister that you have to deceive him or pretend you're going to be a career girl?'

Davina did not answer. He was deliberately confusing her, making her aware of the inadequacy of her carefully laid plans.

'What about your father?' she retaliated. 'Don't you think he'll know immediately? I'm not the sort of girl you ever go out. . . .' She stopped in embarrassment.

'Quite right,' Jake's voice was tinged with humour, 'you're not the sort of girl I normally take out. That's precisely why my father is going to believe in our engagement.'

'Well, what about my job? What happens to that? We can't have a phoney engagement at work. Everyone would know it's a joke.'

'Yes, I agree with you,' Jake said thoughtfully. 'In London we would have no need to keep it up. At work we would return to our normal relationships. You're too valuable to me at the agency to risk your leaving for personal reasons.'

Davina sat quietly trying to gather her scattered wits. Why, she thought, doesn't he ask Andrea Temple to do this for him? Why me? Perhaps because Andrea Temple might have hopes of actually becoming Mrs Jake Humphries, and obviously he was in no rush to get married, to her or to anyone else.

'I can't do it,' she said eventually. 'I could never go through with it. It's too ridiculous. . . . I don't like to lie to my own family or your father.'

'My father you don't even know,' Jake argued, 'and your family you're planning to lie to in any case. At least this way they might believe it and be comforted by our relationship. That's the point of this, isn't it? That your father is comforted, reassured?' He glanced across at her, his head back and eyes veiled in the arrogant stance she knew so well. 'I assure you,' he drawled, 'I'll be able to convince him of my care for your happiness and welfare.'

Davina blushed at his tone.

'It would be a definite . . . er . . . business arrangement, nothing personal?' she asked bluntly, looking straight into his face.

'You have my word on that,' he said quietly, all mockery gone from his face.

'What if you met someone you really wanted to marry?' she asked. 'How would you handle that?'

'I would ask you to release me as I would release you if you found someone you wanted to be free for. This is only a temporary measure, one that will benefit us both for a time.' He sighed wearily. 'You see, for me this is only to help my father face this operation. I want him to go into that certain I've chosen a life partner. After that, who knows. . . .'

'Very well,' she was achingly tired now, 'I'll think it over.'

'You have precisely five minutes,' he said coldly.

'What?' she could feel her hackles rising again at his arrogant attitude.

'Don't be childish, Davina,' said Jake in his normal office voice. 'This has to be decided now, tonight. How else can we make arrangements to go down to your family tomorrow?'

'Oh, dear, I'd forgotten that. . . .' She decided. 'Well, I don't think I can accept, thank you. I just couldn't cope with it all.'

He didn't answer directly.

'Your family live near St Ives,' he said, musing idly, 'and my home is in Mevagissey, less than thirty miles away. I shall be going home tomorrow and so will you. And our homes are within an hour's drive of each other.'

She gasped and stared at him wide-eyed. What an extraordinary coincidence! She wished she knew what was

best. She was so tired and couldn't concentrate ... first
the sherry, then the fire and the meal....

'Let me make the decision for you, Davina. I assure
you you won't regret it. If you give me the name of the
escort agency I'll leave a message on their answering
machine and cancel the arrangement you have with them.
In the morning I'll pick you up and we'll have a leisurely
drive down to the West Country. If you do have second
thoughts you can always continue by train, and we'll have
plenty of time to sort out the details on the way ... what
do you say? Will you trust me and accept?'

She felt a sudden yearning to end all this discussion
and go to bed. She was desperately tired and worn out
with her own feelings and all the talk.

'Very well,' she heard herself say, 'I agree.'

Davina was in the hall promptly next morning.
Discarding the jeans she had planned to wear for the drive
down, she had chosen instead a rose-coloured brushed
cotton dress and matching jacket. It was full-skirted, tight-
waisted and embroidered with tiny white daisies round
the scalloped neck and hem. White sandals, a short black
fur jacket over her arm and carrying her case, she was
ready.

Jake looked cool and remote, with nothing of the
friendliness of the night before. Taking her case with a
brief, 'Good morning, you didn't oversleep, then,' he led
her to the car.

Looking at the sleek lines of the silver blue Rolls,
Davina though how well the large car suited his height.
She thought also of how impressed her family would be
when they saw it.

He wasted no time. Her luggage and fur went into the
boot and within minutes they were on their way. In the
closeness of the car Davina could scent his aftershave, and
it reminded her of the way he had held her the previous
night, easing her pain and giving her comfort. Yet this
morning his face was set and he looked grim, although
dressed for a holiday, in a brown suede jacket with cream

slacks and toning shoes, his silk cream shirt open at the neck his signet ring and gold wrist watch gleaming in the car interior.

Looking at his face, she wondered if he had slept badly. Perhaps he now regretted the arrangement they had made only hours earlier. Maybe he wished he was alone, or perhaps with Andrea Temple. She thought of the lovely elegant girl and wondered if he had planned to have her along today.

Turning her head to look out of the window, she noticed they were heading into town instead of making for the motorway. The car crossed Grosvenor Square and stopped outside the Connaught Hotel. For one awful moment she thought perhaps they were picking up Miss Temple and that she was coming with them, then she dismissed that as a stupid thought, and followed Jake as he ushered her out of the car and into the hotel, tossing the keys to the commissionaire on the way.

Inside they were obviously expected. They were led into the dining room and within minutes Davina found herself at a corner table heavy with white linen and silver cutlery, staring at an enormous menu.

'Right,' Jake said briefly, 'breakfast, I think, don't you? I don't imagine you had any before you came out, and I certainly didn't.'

Davina looked round at the few tables that were occupied so early and noted unseen guests eating or waiting behind enormous newspapers while waiters moved noiselessly across the thick carpet.

'They do a very good breakfast here.' Jake was suddenly cheerful and she listened in awe as he ordered a three-course meal, starting with cereals and seemingly going right through the menu.

Davina asked for coffee and toast and was ignored.

'Let me see,' he sighed, 'madame will have fresh orange juice, scrambled eggs on toast with fresh tomatoes. And we'll have a large pot of coffee with hot milk for two.'

The food arrived on chafing dishes, hot and fragrant, the toast folded into white napkins, the coffee in heavy silver, and they ate in silence.

Davina found she was quite hungry, having downed only a quick cup of instant coffee at home. She enjoyed the food, relieved she was not called on to make conversation.

An hour later they were in front of the hotel and the commissionaire was handing them into a taxi. Jake said nothing by way of explanation and she knew him well enough, in this mood, not to ask a lot of questions.

They travelled down Bond Street, where shops were just opening and stopped outside Cartier. Davina made no move to get out, thinking he must be collecting something, but he reached for her and she found herself on the pavement as he rang the Cartier bell. Once more they were expected. Davina had a quick impression of intense quiet, sparkling glass surfaces, crystal chandeliers shimmering and deep carpets underfoot. They were ushered to a low table at the back of the showroom. She was mystified. She thought again Jake must be collecting a present for someone, and waited patiently.

It was not until two young men carried in a collection of trays, sparkling with rings of all sizes, shapes and stones, that she realised why they had come. She turned to Jake, dismay and embarrassment on her face.

'Please,' she whispered, 'I don't want ... I really can't. . . .'

'Just leave this to me,' he interrupted her coldly. He then asked for the rings to be left for them to sort through alone. With smiles and bows, they were left alone.

Jake drew one of the trays towards them and began to study the rings casually, while she sat petrified and wanting to be gone. He spoke to her quietly.

'Now don't make a fuss, Davina, there's a good girl.'

'Please,' she interrupted, 'I can't possibly wear anything like this! It's far too valuable. I have the ring I bought myself. That's all I need and all I want.'

'I think you must let me be the best judge of that,' he said, his voice hard. 'My father wouldn't be fooled for a moment with the kind of ring you're wearing. It's not the ring I would give my bride.'

She flinched slightly at the word 'bride' and lowered her eyes to hide her blushes. 'Oh, dear. . . .' she said eventually.

'Precisely,' he drawled. 'Just regard it as an investment for me. When we . . . er . . . end our arrangement, you can give it back to me if you feel so strongly about it. And it will be insured. So let's just leave it at that, can we, without more arguments?'

Davina looked at the dazzling display in front of her and wondered how she would feel if Philip was choosing a ring for her. She had sent his back to him, and he had never written, never acknowledged her letter. It had been a very different one from these, just a narrow gold band with one diamond surrounded by seed pearls, and she had loved and treasured it.

'What about this one?' Jake picked up a large square-cut diamond set on a platinum band. 'All women want diamonds, don't they?' he said rather cynically. 'The bigger the better.'

He slipped it on her finger and Davina went cold with fear and revulsion. What was she doing here, pretending to be engaged to someone she hardly knew and she didn't love? How had she got herself into this? She felt the tears rise in her throat and fought off the panic that threatened to engulf her. She had to get out of there and away from Jake. She couldn't go on with this masquerade.

'Davina,' Jake's voice was startled, 'are you all right?' He looked at the whiteness of her face and the tense set of her lips as she tried to control her panic.

'Please,' she whispered, 'I want to go . . . please . . . I can't. . . .' She made to rise, but he stopped her, and she looked up to see his eyes grim and bleak, all laughter and mockery gone.

'I should have known. . . .' he murmured. He flicked his fingers and asked for a brandy and a glass of water for madame, explaining about the heat.

Davina hardly heard what was happening. She drank the ice cold water and felt the panic subside. Jake held out the brandy to her, but she refused with a shake of the head. Then he began to talk to her in a low voice, picking up the rings describing each one, putting it down again, making no move to look at her again, giving her time to regain her composure. She was grateful to him for his understanding and her fears and trembling began to subside.

'You know, it's a funny thing,' he was saying in his normal office voice, 'but I feel your stone isn't really the diamond. Diamonds are glittering, of course, and can be fabulous, but somehow the green of the emerald seems more your stone. It's also beautiful, luminous but softer ... like you,' and he turned and smiled at her. 'What about this one?' He held it out to her. It was quite lovely— a plain square emerald, pale translucent green, set on a white gold band and shimmering in the light from the chandeliers. She looked at him and smiled tremulously.

'Try it on,' he said gently.

It fitted perfectly, and she liked the slightly heavy feel it gave to her hand. 'Do you like it?' she turned shyly to Jake to see if he approved.

He was looking down at the ring, and picked up her hand, holding it lightly in his dark square one.

'It's just you,' he said simply, and stood up.

Davina was given a box for it in a tiny Cartier carrier bag, and they left to find another taxi waiting for them outside.

Back in the Rolls Jake concentrated on driving and they were out of London far more swiftly than she could ever have managed. On the motorway the big powerful car ate up the miles. It was Slough before Jake spoke again.

'After Reading I'm going to take it easy,' he said casually. 'We'll come off the motorway and take the smaller roads. Then we can make detours if we wish.' He looked down at her in sudden brilliant good humour and smiled 'There are magazines and newspapers in the back, or you can adjust your seat and go to sleep,' he said.

It was a luxury for her to be driven instead of driving

herself, and she liked the power of the car and the comfort and ease with which it travelled. As they reached Reading the sun came out, watery at first, and then gradually dispersing the clouds and wind. Jake opened the sun roof and Davina sat, just drifting in and out of her thoughts.

From time to time she would glance out at a village or town as they passed, at cows and horses in the fields, and at distant sun on trees just bursting into bloom. Or she would lie back looking through the sun roof at the clouds blowing by overhead.

It was strange, looking back; she had never been at ease with Jake Humphries. She had always admired and respected him, and at times been more than a little afraid of him. His strongly dominant personality, his good looks and his tremendous virility had always kept her at a distance, slightly withdrawn. She could not share the easy camaraderie that Mike and Charlie enjoyed with him. Even Heather occasionally joined in teasing and backchat with him. Georgina, too, had been genuinely fond of him, and had often fended off young secretaries in the agency, eager to dally with messages in the hope of a word with the eligible and attractive Jake Humphries. Since Davina had taken over Georgina's job several girls had tried to pump her about Jake's private life. But she had always refused to be drawn into any discussion about her boss.

The rare visits to the office of one of his girl-friends had always kept her tonguetied. They were all beautiful, exquisitely dressed, and appeared devoted to him. None of them were very young, she guessed, and none seemed to last very long. But she never speculated about that, and had no interest in his private life. And now, unexpectedly, she was flung right into that private life. And she was not at all sure she would be able to handle this strange relationship they had started so lightheartedly.

But for the moment she was relaxed and content. And there was something more. She felt a strange sense of companionship that she had never found with him at the office, and that she could not remember feeling with anyone else. He was making no demands on her, seemingly content to drive, leaving her to her thoughts with no need to talk.

'We've just passed Shepton Mallet,' Jake's voice intruded into her thoughts. 'Would you like to have lunch at Glastonbury?'

The question, she knew, was merely a formality. Glastonbury was where they would stop for lunch.

'Mm. . . .' she said vaguely.

'I need a break,' he went on, 'and the Pilgrims Inn will give us a light meal. When I'm driving I don't like a heavy meal. It makes me sleepy.'

They parked in the square at the back of the twelfth-century inn and walked through the rear entrance. Davina watched Jake bend his head to avoid the top of the low doorway. They sat in the main room, by the latticed bow windows overlooking the main street of the old town. Dark beams held up the low ceiling and oak trestle tables lined the walls. The bar was housed behind a gleaming brass grille at the back and a pleasant fire burnt in the huge brick fireplace, taking the chill off the day.

Davina chose a home-made vegetable soup followed by a salad with freshly baked bread, and Jake had the special steak and kidney pie. He sighed contentedly as glasses of iced white wine appeared for them both.

'You're a restful girl, Davina Richards, do you know that?' he smiled, and began to tell her something of the inn.

The Benedictine monks of the Abbey had been famous throughout Europe, and pilgrims came in a constant stream throughout the year. The monks had not the room to put up their many visitors in their own quarters, and so the inn became a stop over for these travellers. Each room still carried a famous name from those days.

After lunch they decided to stretch their legs, and wandered round the ruins of the abbey. Jake told her how the Holy Grail had been brought to England by Joseph of Arimathea, who had buried it and founded the first Christian church, according to later chroniclers. The

burial place of the Grail had been marked with Joseph's
staff, and had turned into a holy thorn that blossomed
every Christmas Eve until Cromwell's men cut it down
four centuries later.

The Abbey became rich and famous; one of its most
prestigious Abbots was Henry Blois, Bishop of Winchester,
who used to entertain in royal style. In his time there
were sixty acres of land attached to the Abbey. The last
Abbot was hanged by Henry VIII in 1538 at the time of
the Dissolution of the Monasteries and the king's divorce
and marriage to Anne Boleyn.

They wandered over the grass, looking at the awesome
remains of the Abbey, hinting at its grandeur. The only
building intact was the Abbot's kitchen, and Davina was
thrilled to think how old was the round-domed, square-
based stone building. Inside four huge ovens were built
one into each corner of the kitchen, each with its own
chimney rising in a great pyramid to the roof above.

Jake showed her where the monks had discovered the
graves of King Arthur and Guinevere and thought at the
time they had found Avalon of Round Table fame.

Climbing down into the ruins of the once famous cellars,
Davina slipped. She jumped, trying to save herself, and
fell heavily against Jake as he turned below. His arms
closed tightly round her and she felt the heat of his body
through his thin silk shirt. Her breath came in a gasp and
a sharp tremor of awareness shot through her at his closeness. But a moment later she was free and he had turned
away, going on ahead.

'I think it's time we went on,' he said briefly, and they
headed back to the car. But, strangely, the easy companionship of the day had gone.

'Davina ... come on, Davina, wake up.' The voice
seemed to come from a great distance as she struggled out
of a deep sleep to find herself with her head against Jake's
shoulder. She drew away sharply, blushing selfcon-
sciously.

'We're about a mile from St Ives, and I thought you

might like to titivate before we get there,' he said coldly.

'Oh, yes, thank you, I would.' Her voice was breathy and nervous at the thought of what lay ahead.

'Right,' he opened the car door and got out, 'I'm just going to stretch my legs for a minute, and then we'll move on.'

Davina straightened her clothes, tidied her hair and refreshed her lipstick. They bypassed St Ives and she directed him to Cornish Bay, leaning forward eagerly to note the familiar landmarks, her worries forgotten in the excitement of coming home.

They passed the old mill and sighted the church, turning a corner to face the cottage that Philip used to rent. She wondered if he had kept it on, but doubted it. There was no sign of anyone about. The gate had been repaired, she noticed, and the outside painted. Looking back she could just make out some washing hanging out in the garden.

'Philip's cottage?' Jake's voice was sardonic.

'Yes.'

Her hands clenched in an effort to stay cool, suddenly overwhelmed by what lay ahead of her, and she didn't notice Jake's quick glance at her whitened face. Then they were travelling slowly down her road and there was the house . . . home. The warm stone house with its trailing ivy, the coloured spring flowers and the cherry tree at the gate in full blossom, made her throat ache with sudden homesickness and fear, clammy, panic-stricken fear.

'I can't . . . I want to . . . I don't think. . . .'

'Davina!' Jake's voice was sharp. 'You're here and you're going to face it. You can't run a second time. Come on, girl, pull yourself together.'

His impersonal, cold tone steadied her.

'Yes, of course,' she said bleakly, 'you're quite right.'

Jake opened the car door and turned to her.

'Did you ring and tell them about me?' he asked.

'Oh, no, I forgot. . . .'

'Never mind,' he smiled sardonically, 'the shock of that should take their minds off . . . er . . . other things.'

As he walked round to the boot, the front door opened and her mother came out. 'Darling,' she called, 'I wasn't sure if it was you. ... Oh!' she threw her arms round Davina. 'Oh, it's so wonderful to see you! Welcome home, my love.'

'Mum.' Davina's voice was unsteady, her smile a little tearful.

'I'm so thankful you've come,' her mother whispered with tears in her eyes. 'Now let me look at you.'

As her mother held her at arms' length, Davina noticed how very frail she looked. The blonde hair was almost totally grey, and the face looked smaller and more lined than she remembered. Only the eyes were the same, a little watery at the moment, but still that intense blue.

'Well, I can see you've grown up,' her mother's voice was firmer, '. . . so elegant and so beautiful!'

She turned as Jake came through the gate carrying Davina's case and jacket. He had waited deliberately, Davina guessed, while mother and daughter greeted each other.

Davina turned too. 'Mum,' she said hesitantly, 'this is Jake . . . Jake Humphries——' Her voice failed her and she stopped.

'The man who's finally persuaded her to get married,' Jake smiled at her mother, and once more Davina saw the charm at work. 'I'm sorry,' he said, 'this will come as rather a shock, but I'm hoping in time you won't be displeased.'

'Oh, what a surprise!' Her mother's face was a study in relief, pleasure and some curiosity. 'Well, you naughty girl,' she turned to Davina, 'why didn't you write and let us know? Anyway, why are we standing here? Come inside, both of you.' She walked in, keeping one arm round Davina. 'Welcome,' she said to Jake in the hall.

Davina felt nervous coming into the house. She wondered if Monica and Philip were about. Her father, she guessed, would be at work.

'I'm all alone,' her mother said, answering her unspoken question, 'and I was just thinking of making a cup of tea. I'll do that and then we can decide how to accommodate you both.'

'Oh, no please,' protested Jake. 'I have my own arrangements. But I would love a cup of tea, and so would Davina, I'm sure, but then I must be on my way. My father is expecting me. My home is in Mevagissey.'

'How lovely!' her mother enthused. 'You're so near,' she smiled up at him. 'Well, we'll hear about it all very soon. My husband is still at work, and Monica and her fiancé have gone into St Ives. She's at the hairdresser's, and they're stopping at the church on the way back . . . for a final word with the vicar, I think. Now you must excuse me, I'll go and put the kettle on.'

She bustled off to the kitchen, and Jake put down Davina's suitcase and followed her mother.

The house looked just the same, Davina thought, except it seemed smaller than she remembered, and the hall carpet was a little more worn. She could see into the living room where she noticed new covers on the sofa, and her mother's plants were still everywhere, on tables, hung in baskets and standing in corners on the floor. The kitchen was always Davina's favourite room in the house. Facing south with large windows and a door to the garden, it was a real old farmhouse kitchen with a huge scrubbed wooden table and pretty china on the Welsh dresser along one wall. Her mother was busy with cakes and cups while Jake leaned comfortably against the open door.

'Come along, love, take the tea things through.' Mrs Richards picked up the tray.

'Oh, can't we have tea in here?' Jake pleaded. 'It's so cosy. I do love tea in the kitchen.'

Davina looked at him open-mouthed, but said nothing, and they sat round the table, Jake quite at home as he tucked into her mother's fruit cake.

'I see now where Davina gets her looks, Mrs Richards,' Jake said seriously.

Davina blushed and gave him a furious look. He was really setting out to charm her mother. Well, she'd certainly put a stop to that!

'As you can see, Mum,' she said coolly, 'Jake's a great flatterer.'

'Not at all,' Jake came back smartly, 'I just enjoy being surrounded by beautiful women. Davina tells me her sister is another.'

There was a moment's tense silence, and Davina was at a loss for words. What was he playing at?

'I'm very lucky with my girls. Some mothers have problems if one daughter is less attractive than another. But both mine are gorgeous, and each in a totally different way. You'll see when you meet Monica what I mean, Mr Humphries.'

'Jake, please,' Jake directed one of his deliberate crooked smiles at her mother, who dimpled back at him in delight.

'Very well . . . Jake,' she said. 'They both have a pretty strong will, but Ina of course is the determined one with all the ambition and determination. It's because of her red hair. She has it from her father.'

'Ina?' Jake asked, eyebrows raised.

'Oh, hasn't she told you about that?'

'No. She's kept that very dark.' Jake looked across at her and winked broadly. Davina gave him a furious glare in return.

'Well——' her mother was going to launch into a family anecdote. Davina could see it coming, 'when Davina was born Monica was nearly six, but she couldn't pronounce Davina, and shortened it to "Ina", and somehow it stuck. She was only called Davina when it was punishment time.'

'That I'm sure didn't happen often,' Jake laughed delightedly.

'Don't mind me,' Davina said coldly. 'Perhaps you'd rather I left so that you can discuss all the finer drawbacks in my character.'

Jake leaned across the table and flicked her cheek with one finger. 'You mustn't mind us, love. It's only those we love that we bother to tease. Isn't that right, Mrs R.?'

Davina looked down in embarrassment as the other two

laughed, delighted with each other.

'Hello ... anyone home?' It was her sister's voice in the hall. 'It sounds like the merriment is coming from the kitchen. Let's go and see, darling, what's going on, shall we?'

CHAPTER FOUR

THIS was the moment Davina had been dreading. In one swift movement Jake was in the chair at her side, an arm draped casually about her shoulders. And then Monica was suddenly there in the doorway with Philip just behind her. Davina clenched her hands in her lap, trying to control her features, and she lifted her eyes to her sister's face as she forced herself not to look at Philip. Monica stood rigid with shock, her face grim, her smile dying as she saw her sister.

Jake stood up, keeping his hands possessively on Davina's shoulders.

Mrs Richards broke the tension.

'Darlings!' she trilled, only slightly nervous. 'You're just in time for a cup of tea. Davina's here, as you can see—with a lovely surprise!' She turned to Jake. 'Jake, this is my other daughter, Monica, and her fiancé Philip Andrews. Children, you'll never guess . . . this is Jake Humphries, Davina's fiancé!'

Philip came into the room and Jake straightened up. For a moment the two men looked at each other. Neither said a word. Philip was tall, but Jake topped him by almost a head. The two men nodded briefly to each other, and everyone settled down round the table.

'May I felicitate you, Miss Richards, and wish you every happiness,' Jake said courteously. He sat down again next to Davina, one arm casually round her waist.

'Thank you.' Monica's relief at her mother's announcement had been almost comical. 'Now it's my turn to congratulate you,' she said smilingly to Jake. Davina found herself sitting opposite Philip and looked up to see his eyes burningly intent on her face. Feeling embarrassed at his scrutiny while her sister was there, she turned to look at Monica.

She seemed much the same, vivacious, attractive, her dark curly hair stylishly arranged for tomorrow's wedding, and still slim as she had always been, in spite of her pregnancy. It was only round the blue eyes and the mouth that Davina could see tension and something close to discontent. The mouth was more grimly set than it used to be, and the tiny network of lines round the eyes was more deeply etched. She looked up suddenly to find Davina's eyes on her, and Davina was amazed to see a quick flash of strong emotion in her sister's face, almost like hatred. Her fingers tensed, and she felt Jake's hand close over hers, holding it lightly, almost absentmindedly, his thumb rubbing gently across her wrist. The warmth from his hand penetrated her cold fingers, and she relaxed, unconsciously leaning against him. Looking up, she found Philip's eyes fixed on her, his face white, nostrils flared and his eyes dark with emotion.

'Oh, dear God,' she thought, 'I can't go through with this. Here I am held by one man when the one I love is sitting opposite, engaged to my sister.'

He hadn't changed. She noted the unruly blond hair and ached to put up her hands and smooth it down. He was still breathtakingly handsome, his eyes a deep blue under the firmly arched brows, a short nose, beautiful white teeth. Only his mouth seemed slightly more slack, the lower lip more pronounced than she remembered. Her mother was still talking.

'. . . . Then the wedding is at two in the village church and the reception at the Cornish Castle hotel. . . . After that everyone will come back for a rest, and in the evening there's a dinner dance again at the hotel, a present from Philip's parents. Monica and Philip will be staying at the hotel tomorrow night and fly out for their honeymoon the next day. So you must come to any or all of that as you can. Oh, dear, I am looking forward to introducing you to everyone, Jake . . . oh, and will your father be able to come? It would be lovely if he could.'

'Unfortunately, no. He's not too well at the moment. He'll be sorry to miss it.'

'Well,' her mother said, 'we must make sure to send him some cake.' She turned to the girls. 'Now I must leave you and get on. I've still a few things to get through before your father gets home.'

As soon as she had gone Jake broke into the awkward silence, looking down at Davina.

'I'm afraid, darling, I have to be going too.'

Suddenly Philip spoke. 'You're looking well, Davina,' he said flatly.

'Thank you, Philip.' She raised her head and looked at him calmly. 'So are you.'

'London must suit you,' he went on.

'Yes, I like it. I have friends, a good job and a flat of my own, and I enjoy it all.'

'Oh.' Philip sounded surprised. 'You two aren't ... together, then?' he asked blandly.

She felt Jake stiffen.

'We're engaged, not married,' he said coolly.

'I always thought the permissive society was everywhere in London.' Philip's voice was cold.

'The permissive society is only found among permissive people,' Jake said curtly.

'Oh, dear!' Monica's voice was honey-sweet. 'That does put us in our place, doesn't it, darling?'

Jake pulled Davina to her feet, keeping his arm round her.

'Will you excuse us, please? I must tear myself away. Will you see me out, darling?'

He tightened his hold on her.

'Yes, of course.' Davina moved to the door with him. They both suddenly stopped as Monica gave a loud shriek.

'Philip, have you seen that colossal ring of Davina's? It can't be real, can it? Let's have a look, sweetie.'

Davina flushed bright red as Monica reached for her hand and held it up.

'My God,' Monica breathed in awe, 'it looks like a genuine emerald!' She held Davina's hand up for Philip to see. He seemed mesmerised by the hand and the ring.

'Oh, my, that does put my poor bauble in the shade, doesn't it?' she went on, her voice openly envious. 'Let's have a look at the inscription.'

Jake reached forward quite naturally and took Davina's hand away from Monica, enclosing it in a warm clasp.

'Davina is superstitious about taking it off,' he said lightly, 'and the inscription is very personal.' He smiled charmingly at Monica as he guided Davina out.

In the hall Davina stopped to untangle herself from Jake's hold, her face suddenly chalk white, her eyes dark with pain.

Philip. He still had the power to tear at her heart. She might have an expensive ring that wasn't even her own, but Monica had the man she loved. And she would have given her soul to change places with her sister at this moment. Suddenly the bitterness of it all threatened to overwhelm her.

'Don't look so anguished,' Jake said quietly. 'You're supposed to be in love with me, remember? You can't go into one of your daydreams now, Davina, every time he walks into the room.' He took her by the shoulders and shook her gently.

'I know,' she whispered. They left the house, walking towards the Rolls.

'You may have noticed we're being watched,' said Jake, 'not only from the house, but very likely from the whole road. I can see lace curtains twitching.'

'What are you talking about?' Davina was getting fed up with the whole business and suddenly wished she had never started it.

'I mean, my dear young idiot, if your precious Philip is to believe you're engaged you're going to have to improve very rapidly on your acting performance. At the moment it rates zero. I'm doing all the work. Not that I'm not enjoying it . . . your mother is quite charming, but I do need some help.'

'Well, you look as though you're enjoying it. Smug and self-satisfied would be a good description of your performance!' Davina was seething with anger. 'Our bargain

didn't include making my family fall all over themselves
about you . . . which I'm going to have to cope with when
this farce is over. It looks to me as though you're enjoying
yourself at my expense. Well, I don't appreciate it. And
don't think you can get round me the way you do with
other unsuspecting females, because you can't. I work for
you, remember, and I know what you're really like.'

He stopped quite still and looked at her.

'Well, well, well, the cool, poised, unruffled Davina
Richards showing some spirit at last!' He looked at her
flushed face, her heaving breast and angry eyes. 'I knew
the wilting lily act couldn't last for long.' His eyes glinted
at her. 'Just remember, my girl, you've no reason to feel
sorry for yourself. You're beautiful and intelligent and
gutsy. Your precious ex-boy-friend is the one to feel sorry
for. He's a fool . . . for letting you go, for messing up his
life. And he's stuck with it. You're just waking up from a
long dream, and your life is ahead of you. So don't waste
precious time looking back. He's not worth it.'

They stared at each other as his voice rose triumphantly
to meet her anger. Davina was gripped by a strange excitement she didn't understand, an elation which was
pleasurable and quite new to her.

'And now,' he said calmly reaching for her, 'back to
the performance for the audience.' He pulled her towards
him, tilted her chin with a firm hand and kissed her hard
on the mouth.

She was so surprised, for a moment she didn't move. By
the time she began to pull away, Jake had released her
and was in the car, gears engaged as the Rolls purred
away. One arm out of the window waved at her and the
next moment he had rounded the corner and was gone.

Davina was sitting in front of the dressing table in the
blue guest bedroom, brushing her hair. She had had a
shower, a change of clothes and a rest, when her mother
knocked briefly and came in.

'Hello, love,' she said. 'Had a little rest? I've come for a
chat and to get away from that telephone for a while. It

just never stops ringing!' She sat down on the bed. 'Monica's making a snack supper for us, since the men will be out at the stag party.'

She looked gravely at her daughter, their eyes meeting in the mirror. Davina sensed her mother was determined to be bright and cheerful.

'Little did I think my youngest would turn into such an elegant young woman,' she smiled. 'And yet sitting here now with your hair down, you don't look a day older than . . . when you left,' she finished.

Her voice broke and Davina jumped up. Suddenly they had their arms round each other and were hugging tearfully.

'I really can't believe you're here,' Mrs Richards pulled a handkerchief out of her overall pocket. 'It's been so long and I've missed you so dreadfully.' She sniffed inelegantly. 'There, and I swore I wouldn't cry . . . and anyway, what have I to cry about? One daughter married tomorrow and another engaged. What more could a scheming and ambitious mother want?'

'Oh, Mum, you ambitious and scheming? What a whopper!'

'Now,' Mrs Richards sounded firm and determined, 'you must tell me all about Jake. Where did you meet him? When did you fall in love? How long have you been engaged? When are you getting married? . . . everything,' she laughed.

'Of course, Mum. I'll tell you everything you want to know. But first I want to know about you . . . and Dad.'

Her mother's eyes flew to her daughter's face.

'What do you mean?' She was agitated. 'Has Monica said anything?'

'No, Mum, no one has said anything at all. But you are worried about him, aren't you? Isn't that why I'm here even though Monica obviously doesn't want me to be?'

'Now you mustn't blame Monica too much. I know she can be hard, but don't forget she spent her whole childhood watching your father idolising you. We both suffered with that, and it wasn't easy for her. So you mustn't judge her too harshly.'

They sat close together on the bed.

'Dad's not ill, is he?' Davina said anxiously.

'No, not really, but the doctor has said he has to be careful . . . no more do-it-yourself jobs round the house, only one round of golf a week . . . that kind of thing. There's a heart condition, but nothing to worry about as long as he doesn't upset himself.'

'I see.'

'But he has changed, in the last two years. It's a bit difficult to explain. After you left, he was shattered. He'd always been so proud of you—your achievements, your ambitions, they were somehow an echo of his own youth. And cancelling the wedding like that at the last moment— well, you know how hard it hit me. I made no bones about that at the time. But he didn't say much, and perhaps it hit him much harder than we realised.'

Her mother sighed.

'As you know, he didn't approve of Philip for you, thought you were too young to know your own mind, that Philip had taken advantage of you. But, strangely, his view of Philip changed.'

She looked closely at Davina and paused rather uncertainly.

'I wouldn't be telling you all this if you weren't engaged to Jake and I know you have him to take care of you. When Monica and I sent that invitation we weren't at all sure how you still felt about Philip, you see . . . we thought maybe you wouldn't come because you still. . . .' She laughed lightly. 'Anyway, that doesn't apply any more. As soon as I met Jake I . . . well, it's obvious he's the right man for you and adores you, so . . . you are happy, Davina, aren't you?'

'Yes, Mum, of course I am,' she sounded impatient. 'But go on about Dad.'

'Yes, well . . . he's never really talked about it all even to me, but I think he was surprised when Philip did want to marry you. Somehow he thought Philip would let you down. Then, after the wedding was cancelled, your father saw Philip and realised how much Philip loved you. He did look ghastly, wan and miserable . . . you know.'

Davina winced. Yes, she thought, she did know.

'Anyway, your father became convinced you'd called off the wedding. And Monica agreed with him. And then he turned against you. He didn't want you in the house, didn't want your name mentioned and . . . I had to swear not to write to you or contact you in any way.' She was openly crying now. 'It was awful!' she sobbed. 'I thought it would pass, it was just the passion of the moment, but it didn't. And if anyone mentioned your name . . . you know, the aunts would be here and would ask . . . well, he went mad, shouting, banging doors . . . not like himself at all.'

Davina sat grim and silent. The hurt was sudden and painful. So her father had not believed her that the decision to cancel the wedding had been mutual between her and Philip. He had guessed it was her decision. But did he know anything more? She hoped not, and she determined whatever happened over the week-end he would not know.

'What did he say about my coming this week-end?' Davina asked at last.

'Oh, he agreed. We couldn't have sent you the invitation without that. But . . . well. . . . grudgingly. Oh, darling,' her mother was contrite, 'I don't want to hurt you, but it's better you know before you see him. I wanted to warn you to avoid your being shocked as well . . . as hurt. . . .' Her voice tailed off miserably. 'Perhaps,' she went on, 'seeing you and meeting Jake will change his attitude. He might just come round, don't you think so?' she said eagerly.

'I don't know, Mum. We'll just have to see. Thanks for telling me,' said Davina dispiritedly.

It was all turning out much more complicated than she had imagined, and the whole arrangement with Jake had turned out to be quite unnecessary. Her father wasn't in the least concerned with her happiness.

'But, Mum, how is he taking the wedding?'

'Yes, well . . .' her mother said again, 'he doesn't know, of course, that there's a baby on the way, and he doesn't know either that they've been living together in London. He thinks Monica has a job in London, which she has, of course, and that they met up again there and fell in love.'

Davina wondered suddenly how much of the real truth her mother knew. Did she know what happened between herself and Monica that evening two years ago? Somehow she doubted it. But it wasn't important.

Oh, God, she thought, what a muddle!

'I wish I hadn't come,' she now said to her mother.

'No, don't say that. I wanted you to come because your father needs you. Once Monica is married, he'll need you even more. Whatever is between you must be sorted out. As long as you were in London and he never saw you, it couldn't be. I want so much for you both to be reconciled.

'That's another reason I'm so glad about Jake. Your father will see now that you're happy and settled and that there's no more feeling between you and Philip. That may help. I think perhaps he's been a bit afraid that Philip might still . . . well, that he might still feel rather strongly about you. I know Monica's been afraid of that too. But of course all that's behind us, so it's good that you're here. . . .' She paused. 'And I don't think I could have gone on much longer without you once Monica was married and gone.'

Davina looked penetratingly into her mother's face. 'You haven't had an easy time, have you?'

'Well, perhaps not. These last two years haven't been the best. But there are always good times and bad . . . you just remember that, young woman, when you're married.'

The phone shrilled downstairs.

'Oh, dear, I do hope Monica hears that.' Mrs Richards sounded doubtful.

It stopped and then came her father's voice in the hall, 'Anybody home?' and the closing of the front door.

'There's your father now. I must go down.'

'Alison, where are you?'

Her mother turned at the door. 'You will be . . . patient with your father, won't you?' she asked anxiously.

'Don't worry, Mum, it'll be alright. I'm not a schoolgirl any more, you know!' They smiled at each other and her mother went.

Davina wished she could get an old coat and go on to the dunes for a walk, give herself time to think out everything her mother had said. But she knew she would have to stay and see her father.

The phone rang again. At least, she thought wryly, there would not be much time for problems over the weekend. They would all be much too busy.

'Davina!' it was Monica's voice. 'It's for you.'

Davina went out on to the landing. 'Who is it?'

'I don't know. Can you come down and get it? I'm just in the middle of something for Mum.'

'Yes, of course . . . coming,' she called down.

Monica's voice sounded suddenly quite normal, and Davina's spirits lifted. Whatever was ahead she was happy to be home, to see her family again. She had not realised in London how terribly she missed it all.

She ran down the stairs, taking the last three in one leap as she always used to do, and felt her depression lift away from her.

'Hello,' she said cheerfully into the phone.

'That sounds better, much better.' It was Jake's voice.

'Oh, it's you.' She sounded serious again.

'Well, don't sound so disappointed. I rang to ask if you could come with me in the morning to buy a wedding present.'

Davina thought for a moment. 'I'm not sure. There may be things for me to do here.'

'It doesn't have to be early. Around eleven.'

'They won't be expecting a present, Jake. There's no need.'

'I realise that, but I don't want to arrive with another toast rack or a third glass bowl.' He paused. 'If you could look the presents over this evening, I'd know what to get.'

'O.K.,' she said, reluctant to commit herself. 'I'm still not sure.' She wondered why he was being so persuasive.

'Good. I'll pick you up at eleven sharp.'

'I haven't said I'll come yet.'

'You're only hesitating in case more exciting invitations come up,' he said cryptically.

'That's rubbish,' she retorted rather too forcefully.

'I thought so,' Jake said mockingly, and hung up.

She stood for a moment, realising she hadn't asked after his father.

'Davina!'

She turned to see her father standing in the doorway watching her. She felt a sudden rush of happiness at the sight of him and flew towards him. But she slowed down before she reached him as he did not open his arms to her as he used to do. She stopped. 'Hello, Dad,' she said carefully.

His voice was formal. 'You look wonderful, my dear. Quite grown up and even more lovely.'

'Thank you.' She was near to tears. 'It's good to be home.' She was trying hard to hide her disappointment as they walked into the living room.

'Your mother and I are happy to have you here on such an important day.' His voice was almost stilted.

Davina down on the sofa, feeling suddenly weak.

'Can I offer you a drink, my dear?'

'I'll have a sherry, please, if you have it!'

'We may live in the back of beyond, but we do have sherry.' His voice was dry and slightly bitter.

Davina laughed lightly, determined not to show her hurt at his attitude. 'I may look different, Dad,' she said slowly and deliberately, 'but I haven't changed underneath.'

'Let's hope devoutly that that's not true. There were some things two years ago that could well do with changing.'

She bit her lip, realising how right her mother had been to counsel patience. As he brought her glass, she looked at him carefully. He had aged even more than her mother.

His hair, now receding from his forehead, was completely white at the sides. His eyes, so much like her own, were cool and impersonal as he looked down at her. The lines round his mouth were deep and darkly shadowed, with new furrows on his forehead as he frowned heavily.

This was not the father she remembered. Her mother had said he had idolised her, but not more than she had adored him. His rejection of her had hurt more than she cared to admit to her mother.

'As your mother will have told you, we've been muddling through here without you,' he told her. 'Nothing much has changed. Monica has chosen wisely and has given herself time to be sure of her own feelings, as I once advised you to do. Her feelings have stood the test of time.'

Davina breathed in deeply to clear the constriction in her throat. 'Everyone seems to have worked very hard to make tomorrow a really lovely day,' she said brightly, 'and I'm looking forward to unpacking presents with Monica later.'

'Just as hard as we worked for your wedding,' he remarked tonelessly.

'I hope, Dad, we'll be able to put all that behind us and look forward.' She was fighting the tears threatening to spill from her lashes. 'I'm sure that's what Monica and Mum would wish for her wedding day. Don't you think so?'

He turned his back to her to look out at the garden.

'Not all of us can forget that easily, Davina, even if you can,' he said deliberately.

Davina took a deep breath. 'Dad. . . .' she began.

'Your mother tells me,' he interrupted harshly, 'that you're thinking of marriage again.' He turned round to look at her, but she said nothing. 'I hope this time you've chosen more wisely,' he said. 'I trust also you've been honest with him and told him of your . . . er . . . regrettable weaknesses.'

Davina gasped, 'Whatever do you mean?'

'Your tendency to grab what you want doesn't usually

make for lasting happiness. Last time you couldn't wait for marriage and Philip allowed you to persuade him to anticipate your wedding night. And then you found you didn't want him after all, and you hurt him badly. Your sister hasn't made the same mistake. She had the patience to wait. I hope you've learned from your mistake. Men don't always respect what they can have too easily. Another time such a course of action might backfire on you—the man might not want to marry you afterwards.'

Davina shrank from him. He believed she had had an affair with Philip and found she didn't want him after all? Is that what was behind all this? How could he think that of her when he knew her so well? Had someone told him a lot of lies? Had Monica . . . or even Philip . . . told him this to shield themselves from his anger? Suddenly she was angry, and her anger was stronger than her hurt.

'How can you believe those things of me, your own daughter? What do you know about it? You didn't ask me at the time—you didn't accuse me of all these things. Who's told you all these lies? Who told you what I felt or what I did?'

'I didn't need to be told. I could see it, just looking at you, that last day.'

'That's not fair, and you must know it! Why couldn't you trust me to tell you the truth? Why didn't you tell me of your fears and we could have talked it out?'

'Trust?' His voice was rising dangerously. 'I would have trusted you blindfold to the far corners of the earth. That's what made it worse. You betrayed that trust, mine and your mother's . . . and Philip's. He trusted you, didn't he? But you're paying the price watching him marry your sister. That seems a fitting punishment.' He breathed deeply. 'I can only say it serves you right.'

'No, David, no!' It was her mother's shocked voice from the doorway. 'It wasn't like that. You know all these things aren't true!' She came to his side, putting her arms round him. 'We must put all this behind us now. Please, darling . . . please!'

'I'm sorry, mother,' he said firmly, but more quietly,

'but I can't. I permitted you to invite her today because I know how much it means to you to have her here. But Monica feels with me. She's not sure Davina should be here. Now she's here with my permission, but that doesn't mean I condone what she's done.'

Suddenly Davina's control snapped. She shouted angrily,

'I'm sorry you've condemned me unheard! I would never have believed you capable of that. I'm also sorry you invited me down here. But that can be remedied easily. I'll leave first thing in the morning and take my contaminated presence away from you all!'

'No, Davina no!' It was her mother's voice calling her as she ran out of the room, tears streaming down her face, her control finally broken.

CHAPTER FIVE

AFTERWARDS Davina could not remember how long she wandered or where she had gone. The evening was drawing in when she found herself on the dunes, her feet leading her to the sanctuary she had known in times of trouble since she was a child. The small sheltered cove led through tough, high grass steeply down to a tiny inlet where at high tide the sea lapped on to the rocks. It was too small to be of interest to tourists and was deserted even during the holiday season. In the summer it was a sun-trap where Davina used to sit, her back against the heat of rock and sand, undisturbed for hours on end.

Even Monica did not know of her retreat. Only with Philip had she shared it. Here they would meet to be alone, revelling in the quiet, knowing they would not be disturbed.

She was glad of her serviceable, flat shoes and her warm sweater as she sank down on to her favourite smooth, flat stone and leaned back, letting the sounds of sea, wind and birds wash over her.

Her family life seemed in tatters, and she had never felt so alone. Being lonely in company as she had been sometimes in London was bad. But being alone and lonely when with those one loved seemed much worse.

She should never have come. She had wanted to see them all, and had hoped it would be as it used to be, before all the traumas and emotional upheavals. But she had been wrong. It could never be the same again. She had grown up and away from them. And her father could not forgive her for what he thought had happened. The truth he would never hear from her, and she doubted if Monica would ever tell him everything. So there was nothing for her at home any more. If it wasn't for her mother, she would go now, immediately. All she wanted now was to get away, back to London, to her flat, the sanctuary she should never have left.

If she had come without Jake, she could have got into her car after the wedding ceremony and gone home. But she had involved herself in his life and his plans. That, too, had been a mistake. And she was stranded; she couldn't get away. She had promised him she would go to his father on Sunday, and she couldn't let Jake down; she had given her word.

All the complications from which she had tried to guard herself in her agreement with Jake had come to nothing. It didn't matter to her father if she still loved Philip. He would probably feel even that served her right, having to watch her sister marry the man she loved.

She had made a complete mess of her own life, and now she was doing a bad job trying to protect those she loved. She wondered fleetingly if she could ring Jake, ask him to let her out of the arrangement they had, so that she could go home right away. What would he say? By this time would he have mentioned his 'engagement' to his father? Probably, she guessed.

Her mind went round and round, trying to figure out some way, some solution, but nothing made any sense. There was no help anywhere. And her love for Philip. . . . Wearily she leaned her head back against the rock and closed her eyes. . . .

'Davina . . . a . . . a!'

Someone was calling her. She woke up with a start, feeling the ache in her back where she had rested against a hard rock.

She remembered where she was and listened. Who could be calling her? It was pitch dark and she must have slept for hours. The tide was right out, and she could hear the wind howling, although she was sheltered from its blast. Her body ached all over as the numbness began to wear off, and she felt cold and damp. Painfully she got up and brushed herself down. At least, with the tide out, she could walk home along the sand and escape a climb up the cliff in the dark.

'Davina!' The voice sounded suddenly much closer She could hear the crunch of footsteps in the wet sand, and her heart thudded into her mouth as she recognised that voice.

It was Philip.

Another minute and he was standing inside the tiny cove. She couldn't move. Of course, it had to be him. If they were looking for her he would be the only one who knew where to find her.

She just stood there looking up at him in the bright moonlight as the wind whipped the clouds suddenly clear of the full moon above. At last she could shed the indifference she had pretended when they met earlier in the day, and she drank in the familiarity of his tall figure.

He came forward in two strides and took her hands, looking down into her face. Without a word he took her into his arms.

'If only you know how I've longed for this moment!' he whispered.

Suddenly she shivered in his arms, not knowing why those words sounded ominous.

'You're cold, my lovely,' he said tenderly, the old endearment touching her as nothing else could have done. He pulled her close inside his coat, close to his body for warmth, and she put her arms round him.

'You remembered this place?' she asked.

'How could you ask?' he said.

'Oh, Philip!' Her voice broke into a tender laugh. 'Do you know you haven't changed at all?'

'Ah, but you have, my dearest. You've grown up,' he breathed, his voice low in her ear. 'You're exquisite, and desirable beyond my wildest dreams'. His voice suddenly broke. 'Oh, my darling,' he muttered, and buried his face in her neck. Davina closed her eyes against his hair, suddenly unnerved by his nearness. As his hold tightened, she felt the familiar roughness of his chin and the hair blowing against her cheek. She put up a hand to smooth it, stroking his neck as he murmured to her. 'Oh, how I've missed you, ached for you, for long months wanted nothing but to hold you in my arms, to tell you how much I love you. Why did you leave me, Davina? Why?'

She was leaning against him, loving the security she always felt in his arms, knowing how much he wanted and needed her. That at least hadn't changed. Philip did still love her.

He looked into her face and then bent his head to kiss her, softly at first, gently and then hungrily, his kiss deepening as he felt her response. All the old familiar feelings came back to her as she kissed him, and everything was the same as it had been when they were together. It was as though time had not moved, but waited for them to find each other again.

But suddenly memory returned sharply and Davina wrenched out of his hold. 'No, Philip, no! This is wrong, impossible. Please stop. . . .'

'There's nothing wrong about the way I love you, Davina, adore you. I always have, all this time. And I've wanted you every minute, every day. You don't know how much. Don't deny me this. Let me hold you, please, Davina darling.'

She was tempted to slip back into his arms and feel the warmth of his body and his love, especially when their love for each other seemed the only safe thing in a world gone mad with hate and anger. She controlled herself and stood up straight, her hands at her side. She didn't try to make light of it, or pretend she didn't care.

'It's too late for all that, Philip—we both know that. And there's no point in talking. We must get back.'

'No, Davina, please let me look at you, talk to you for a few minutes. Please, my darling, give me that.'

Suddenly Davina felt inexpressively weary.

'No, Philip. I don't know why you're here, but we must go back, and at once. If someone were to see us together, it would be terrible. Just imagine what Monica would feel.'

'Oh, Monica will know where I am.' His voice was hard with contempt, and she flinched at his tone.

'What do you mean?' she asked.

'She knows how much I love you. She knows I pretend I'm making love to you when she's in my arms.' His voice was bitter and full of some kind of pity for himself, and Davina went cold with fear.

'I don't understand what you're saying, Philip.'

'Don't you? It's just that she knows I don't love her. I love you and I always will.' He broke off and his voice changed to entreaty, 'Please, darling, don't leave me again. I couldn't bear it for a second time. You don't know what it does to me to see you . . .' his voice hardened '. . . to see you with another man's ring on your finger. I could kill him! If he's had you when I . . . oh, but all that doesn't matter any more . . . we've found each other again, and nothing is going to come between us this time.'

Davina went cold at his words. She was finding it difficult to follow what exactly he was saying. This couldn't be Philip, the man she loved, the man she had been faithful to all this time, saying such horrible things, conjuring up pictures that made her feel quite ill. There must be some explanation, and she had to try and understand.

'But you're marrying each other tomorrow. How can you do that when you say you don't love Monica?'

'You might just as well ask how we could have stayed together when she's known all along. I've been honest with her, I've never lied to her or pretended. I wouldn't do that.'

'But, Philip, if that's true how could she be having your baby?'

'You can't still be that much of an infant, my dearest. It's quite possible for a man to take what's being offered and still keep the image of another woman in his heart and mind.'

'Oh, no! No, Philip . . .' she was sobbing now, 'how dreadful . . . poor Monica!'

'Look, Davina, I refuse to talk any more about Monica. Anyway, it's not at all certain she's having a baby. I have no proof. For all I know she's making it all up. She wouldn't let me see the doctor. And it has nothing to do with you and me, and it's you and me I'm interested in.'

Davina recoiled from him. This man in front of her, so familiar, was a total stranger. Perhaps she had never known him at all, never understood him. Perhaps it was she who had changed. But for the first time she felt sorry for her sister, loving Philip and getting such a raw deal from him.

'That's enough, Philip.' Her voice was curt. 'I'm going in now. I don't want you to come with me any further. I'll see you tomorrow in church. But I'm engaged now, and in future you'll be my brother-in-law ... nothing more and nothing else.' She started to walk up the sands away from him, but he stayed by her side.

'I'm an idiot,' he muttered. 'I keep forgetting you don't know what happened. You think me selfish and unfeeling, heedless of your sister's happiness. Well, let me tell you what really happened after you left.'

'No,' Davina said harshly. 'I don't want to hear any more.'

'Well, you're going to listen, Davina Richards. You owe me that at least for the way you ran out on me without asking me for an explanation.'

She was silent. This was true. She had run out on him, taking Monica's word for what had happened between them.

They continued to walk side by side, but Philip made no attempt to touch her.

'After you left,' he said heavily, 'and sent me the ring back, I just wanted to get away from here ... from your family, the job and everyone who knew about us. I gave in my notice and cut all my ties. I wanted nothing round me that reminded me of you, so I went to London. Monica found me there. She'd traced me, and she asked if we could talk, see each other sometimes. I didn't care either way, but I agreed. I explained to her that I still loved you, and that this would not change. Perhaps she didn't believe me. I don't know, but we began to see each other regularly.' His voice changed and became apologetic. 'I was lonely, very lonely. She offered to cook me the occasional meal and then she'd do my laundry on the quiet, without telling me. Before I knew it she had a key to my flat. At first she just stayed the odd few hours in the evenings, and then she offered to clean up for me when I wasn't there and it would be more convenient if she had a key.'

He paused for a moment as Davina increased her pace of walking, still wanting to get away from him, not to listen to what he was telling her.

'Then one evening I came home to find she'd moved in. I pointed out that she was wasting her time, there was no future in her staying with me because I wouldn't marry her. I was in love with you and always would be.' He sighed deeply. 'She said she didn't mind. She wasn't interested in marriage and she'd just stay with me for the time being because it suited her and she didn't have to pay any rent.'

'That wasn't true, of course,' Davina said shortly.

'Probably not. And maybe I should have sent her away. It's easy to have hindsight about these things. . . . Anyway, twice in the next six months she told me she was pregnant, and each time it turned out to be untrue. So when she told me this time I ignored it. But then she told me something else, and that did change things.' Philip stopped, and Davina was held by the sudden seriousness of his tone. She, too, stood still and they faced each other on the moonlit sands.

'She told me you'd got married. She'd told me from the beginning that you'd gone abroad, that you had a travelling job as companion with some woman. But now she said you'd met someone on your travels and were married.' His voice rose harshly. 'Now do you understand why I asked her to marry me? To give the baby a name. I knew this time I'd lost you for good, that there would never be another chance for me. And then nothing mattered very much. I thought I might as well give Monica what she wanted so much. Then when I met your father and he was so pleased . . . much to my surprise . . . we named the day.'

'Monica told you I was abroad?' she whispered into the silence.

'Yes.'

'Is that why you never tried to find me?'

'Yes. If I'd known you were in London, even without your address I would have found you somehow, sometime. And I would have begged you on my knees to forgive me to give me another chance to make you happy, to come back to me. As I'm doing now,' he ended quietly.

Davina said nothing. The only sound in the night was the rhythmic crunching of their feet in the wet sand. She turned away from the beach to the road and headed for home. She was cold and tired. She didn't feel anything, neither elation at Philip's declaration of love nor happiness at the thought that she could run away with him now and marry him if she wanted to do that. There seemed to be no feelings left inside for anything or anyone. Too much had happened too quickly, and she wanted to go to sleep and forget it all. But she knew she would have to make at least one decision immediately. And she knew what it would have to be.

She had her own life, a job, a home and friends, but her sister had nothing. If Philip were to leave her, all she would have would be his illegitimate child. And Davina herself would have a permanent breach with her family for the second time, and for good. However much she loved Philip, she couldn't wreak such havoc or cause so much unhappiness to the people she loved. She might regret it bitterly one day, but for the moment that would have to be the decision.

She turned to Philip at the corner of the road.

'From here on I go alone, Philip. What you've told me . . . well, it might have made a lot of difference once, but not now. Our love ended for me when you had an affair with my sister. That, I notice, you haven't denied. And perhaps, who knows, your marriage to each other might work out after all.' Her voice shook a little. 'There's no way that I'll break my engagement to go away with you, Philip. And that's quite final. Goodbye.'

She turned and walked away without looking back.

The house was dark and quiet when she let herself in, although there was still a light under the door of her parents' room and she could hear their quiet voices. She tiptoed to her own room and dropped into bed, only to find she was too tired to sleep. Tossing and turning, she slipped into a doze between waking and sleeping, dreaming of a home with Philip and herself while everyone looked on in happiness. Only her sister wasn't there and she couldn't find her.

It was early morning before she finally fell into a deep exhausted sleep.

'Davina, wake up! Why have you locked the door? Davina!' It was Monica. 'Will you please open up? I've got a cup of tea . . . come on!'

In one movement Davina was out of bed and unlocking the door.

'Sorry, love,' she said sleepily, 'I must have overslept.' She looked at the clock and glanced in dismay at her sister. 'It can't be ten o'clock! I should be bringing you tea this morning, not have you getting it for me.' She smiled quite naturally at her sister 'Jake is going to be here in an hour, and I've done nothing to give Mum a hand. She must be furious!'

Monica just stood there, holding the tea tray not saying anything. Davina pulled on a dressing gown and took the tray.

'Have you got time to have a quick one with me?' she smiled.

'No', Monica's voice was sullen, 'I've too much to do,' and she turned to the door. But Davina was before her. She closed the door before Monica reached it and turned to face her sister.

'I'm sorry I didn't get back last night to help unpack the presents. . . . Jake particularly asked what you would like. He's very keen to get you something you really want.'

'There's no need for him to get anything,' Monica said

dully, 'although he can obviously afford it. You've done extremely well for yourself, haven't you?'

Davina didn't say anything, but poured a cup of tea.

'I wondered if you had a coffee percolator. You always used to like your coffee percolated.'

'No, we haven't,' Monica said unhelpfully. 'Why didn't you ask Philip last night?'

Davina gasped.

'Did you think it was a dead secret that you went to see him?' Monica asked harshly.

'But I didn't. . . .' Davina began.

Monica interrupted, 'I don't know why you're here. I didn't want you to come. I let Mùm persuade me into writing that invitation.'

'You told Philip I was married,' Davina accused her sister.

'That's right,' Monica snapped. 'You still don't understand anything at all about love, do you? You never loved Philip, only he doesn't know it, and I can see you don't really love your Jake. Perhaps you're just cold and frigid and can never really love anyone. But I love Philip, and I'd do anything to keep him from you . . . lie, cheat, steal, anything. Can you understand that?' Her voice broke. 'Oh, God, why did you have to come back?'

Davina whitened at the hatred in Monica's voice.

'You really do hate me,' she whispered.

'Yes, I do! And the sooner you get away from here, the better I shall like it. I suppose Philip told you a sob-story about how he's marrying me because he feels sorry for me, responsible for the baby I'm going to have.' Monica's voice rose in anger. 'Well, you don't know him, not the way I do. He really does love me. You're just a dream, a fairytale virgin he can escape to in his mind whenever things get rough and real life gets him down. But live with your sanctimonious, pious goodness every day of his life? He'd go nuts! He wouldn't stand it for a week. I'm much more his type than you ever were.' She moved to stand over Davina as she sat on the bed. 'And if poisoning

his mind against you is going to help him realise he loves
me, then that's what I'll do! And now go ... go and
don't come back, ever. We none of us need you any more,
Not even Dad. He loves me now, not you. I'm his favourite, the apple of his eye. And you know what? I like it
that way!'

She raised her voice, the venom in it close to hysteria,
and Davina turned away in horror. Was there to be no
end to the hatred and violence? What had happened to
her family? Where had it all come from? Was Monica
right? Was she herself frigid, cold, unable to love anyone?
She looked at Monica, her eyes expressionless.

'I'm going,' she said quietly. 'If it wasn't for Mum, I'd
go before the wedding, but I can't do that to her.'

'Please yourself.' Monica had quietened down. 'Once
we're married I don't care what you do. Then I've got
him. And I know you ... you'd never take a married
man from his wife.' Her tone was bitter.

'I'm sorry, Monica,' said Davina quietly. 'I'd hoped
we could reach some kind of understanding, you and I.
You're older than I am and more experienced, I know
that. But, even if we'd met during the last two years, I
would never have made mischief between you and Philip.
You should have known that. There was no need to lie to
him about. . . .'

Monica said nothing and turned her back on her
sister.

'Anyway,' Davina went on, 'after today, we don't have
to meet again if you want it that way.'

'You can stay tonight, if you like,' Monica said un-
graciously. 'I don't want Mum upset, and she would be if
you just went off. I don't care if Philip snatches a few
kisses on the dance floor, because by then he'll be mine.
Anyway, your Jake might have something to say about
that. He strikes me as the possessive sort—and overbear-
ing. I wish you joy of him. Give me a man I can wind
round my finger when I need t. I wouldn't want to tangle
with your fiancé.'

'You're not being asked to,' Davina said tartly, more

than a little angry at her sister's tone.

'Do you know, you're just as childish as you were two years ago about men?' sneered Monica. 'You haven't learnt a thing. Well, I can tell you, one doesn't mess about with men like Jake Humphries. I know his type. Once he's got you to love him and do what he wants, he'll be out amusing himself as no doubt he's used to do.'

'It seems to me,' Davina said quietly, 'you have enough on your hands without taking on my fiancé as well.'

'Well, don't say I didn't warn you,' Monica said triumphantly, and flounced out of the room.

Davina sat stunned on the bed, feeling again the urge to run away, from everyone. But she knew that to be impossible. Somehow she had to get through the day ... and tomorrow with Jake and his father. But she was not going to sit and think about it. She had a quick shower and pulled on some tight black jeans with a matching mohair sweater, leaving her hair loose, tied back with a black ribbon, then she ran down to the kitchen to find her mother.

'Good morning, darling.' Her mother was in the kitchen. In an overall with her hair tied into a scarf she looked a little distracted.

'I'm so sorry to sleep so late, Mum. I meant to be down ages ago and give you a hand.'

'Nonsense, this is a holiday for you and it's pretty well all done.' Mrs Richards looked at her daughter rather pointedly. 'Everything all right?' she queried.

'Yes, of course.' Davina's voice was deliberately light and she did not look directly at her mother. 'I just lost my cool last night. I think I must have been a bit tired. But a walk cleared my head.'

'Good.' She could see her mother decided to accept that explanation. 'In that case you must be starving, and I'll cook you some breakfast.'

'No way.' Davina was emphatic. 'All I want is toast and coffee, and I can make some of that myself.'

'Very well, dear,' her mother sounded relieved, 'I'll leave you to help yourself. You won't mind if I'm in and out and not entirely with it?'

Davina lit the grill and cut bread. 'Now tell me what I can do this morning and what exactly is happening.'

'Well, the hairdresser will be here at twelve and will do my hair first. After that he'll be with Monica and do her veil. Then I'll slip into my things and leave for church. After that only Dad and Monica will remain. I think that's about it. Sounds quite simple, doesn't it? I don't know why I'm in such a dither. . . . Your father has locked himself into the study with the presents . . . oh, that reminds me, the best man will be here for those in . . . what's the time? . . . oh dear, in half an hour,' and she wandered off.

Davina was sitting down to her toast when the front door rang. She heard Monica's voice in the hall.

'Jake, what a lovely surprise! Can you find her for yourself? I think she's in the kitchen.'

There was a low murmur from Jake and then her mother. 'Jake, how nice! How are you this morning? And how is your father?'

Another low reply from Jake's deep voice, and then he appeared in the kitchen doorway. He was dressed for the wedding in a pale grey suit of fine mohair with toning silk shirt and darker tie. As always he seemed enormously vital. Davina blinked for a moment, quite tongue-tied at his magnificence and the power he seemed to exude. His look travelled from her sweater down the tight jeans and then up to the silky hair hanging down her back. For a moment he stood quite still just looking at her, then he moved and kissed her lightly on the top of her head.

'Good morning, Cinderella,' he said. 'Are you coming?'

'I . . . was . . . er . . . hoping you wouldn't mind, Jake, if I left you to it. I know what it is they want, and there's an awful lot to do . . . and I'm afraid I overslept, and I've only just come down.'

He looked at her intently, noting her hurried, awkward speech and the pallor of her face. She refused to look at him, keeping her eyes on her toast which she was still spreading rather slowly.

'I see. Well, of course, if you want to stay, I'll manage without you. . . .'

'Certainly not!' her mother interrupted. 'Take her away, Jake, for goodness' sake. She'll only be in the way here. I'll be glad to see the back of her for an hour or two.'

'Well,' Davina looked at her mother, 'that's just great!'

'No, really, darling, everything is done. After all, it's not as though we're having the reception here. Go on, off you go. I'm sure a drive will do you good.'

'Well, I can't go like this with you all dressed up. . . .' Davina blushed.

'Like a dog's dinner?' Jake finished for her. 'Yes, that is a problem, but I'm determined not to let it worry me. So finish your breakfast and let's get going.'

'I'll leave you to it, then. Don't forget, Jake, to have her back in time to change.'

'That's a promise,' he said, and Mrs Richards went off. Jake had not sat down and now he walked over to the window, his back to Davina.

'You look terrible,' he said quietly, and turned back to face her. 'Have you seen Philip?'

'I didn't sleep very well. . . .' she began.

'Spare me the details,' he interrupted, his voice hard. 'Was it the grand reunion you'd hoped for, I wonder?'

Davina said nothing.

'You're a fool, Davina, do you know that?' he said evenly.

'Yes,' she said simply.

'Stop maltreating that toast,' he said curtly. 'I suggest you leave it and we go.' He walked over to the table and picked up her left hand. Absentmindedly he touched the ring he had given her only the day before, looking into its luminous green depths. Deliberately he turned the hand over and bent his head to put his lips firmly against the open palm.

Davina quivered at his touch, but surprise kept her still, while strange sensations were shooting up her arm to her heart and she began to tremble with some kind of weakness. At last the caress ended, and Jake lifted his head to look straight into her eyes. A shaft of feeling seemed to crackle between them as grey eyes looked into grey. Then he straightened, keeping her hand in his, and pulled her up from the table and out.

As they emerged into the hall she stopped. Her father was coming out of the study.

'Good morning, Dad,' she said nervously.

'Good morning, Davina.'

'Dad, I'd like you to meet Jake Humphries. Jake, this is my father.'

'How do you do, sir.' Jake walked towards him with outstretched hand. 'I'm very happy to meet you.'

Her father stood still. He did not take the outstretched hand, and Jake dropped it to his side.

'I was hoping, sir,' he said, 'to have a talk with you, but I realise this week-end isn't a good time.'

Her father spoke at last.

'I understand you and my daughter are engaged to be married.'

'I hope, sir, with your permission. . . .'

'You must know,' Mr Richards interrupted, 'Davina doesn't want to be married. She likes older men, but she doesn't marry them. The last one she liked was old enough to be her father.'

The words dropped like leaden weights into the silence of the hall. Davina fought against a sudden feeling of intense nausea and prayed she would not faint.

'I beg your pardon?' Jake's voice was icy.

Her father replied, his voice cold and indifferent, his face a controlled mask, 'I see you're a man of the world and a good deal older than my daughter. Perhaps you also are old enough to be her father. Older men with a wide experience of women often appeal to young girls. And Davina started young to have love affairs, but unfortunately they never last. Even when she promises marriage, as she has with you, it won't last. She won't marry you. The last man to whom she promised herself in marriage is marrying her sister today.'

'Father, please don't. . . .' Davina's voice died to silence as she realised he had said everything there was to say. He had humiliated her, stripped her of all self-respect. She wanted to run and never come back, never have to see any of them again, but her legs wouldn't carry her. She knew if she took a step she would fall. So she leaned weakly against the wall behind her.

Then Jake spoke, quietly, in a voice of frightening menace.

'Your age, sir, and your relationship to Davina make it impossible for me to deal with you as I would with any other man who had dared to say such things. None of them are true, as I have reason to know. She has integrity and compassion, qualities rare in women of any age, and I pity you that you can't appreciate your own daughter.' He was breathing heavily, his face white, nostrils flared, and Davina realised he was having trouble controlling his anger. 'But even if what you say about her was true and we were having an affair and I was old enough to be her father, it would still not give you the right to speak of her as you have done. If circumstances were different I would take her away and not allow her back until I had your abject apology. But I have too much respect for Mrs Richards to behave so selfishly, and I don't think Davina would let me. Since it's her sister's wedding, we'll be in church and at the reception and at the dance. But I shall be there to protect her from the kind of hurt and humiliation you've inflicted on her here today.'

He turned and walked to the front door.

'I'll wait for you in the car, Davina,' he said quietly, and let himself out.

'Oh, Dad,' she whispered, 'what have you done? And why?'

Her father turned and, without a word or a look, went back into his study, closing the door.

Davina walked unsteadily to the front door and out. The cool breeze against her face steadied her slightly. She closed the door behind her and made for the steps. But suddenly she realised she wouldn't make it. She could feel her legs buckle . . . she knew she would fall and she called out.

Jake must have been watching for her. Before she reached the ground he had leapt up the steps and was beside her, lifting her and carrying her to the car. He put her gently into the front seat, closed the door and got in behind the wheel. Within minutes they were away from the house, Davina leaning back, eyes closed, breathing in gulps of fresh air from the open window.

The car stopped, but she didn't move.

'Drink this,' Jake commanded, holding a flask to her lips.

'No . . .' she said weakly.

'Drink it,' he repeated.

'I'm trying not to be sick,' she whispered.

'This will help. Come on, Davina, don't be silly. It's only brandy.'

She took a little as he tipped the flask to her mouth and the liquid burned her throat, but her head cleared and the nausea passed.

Jake sat back and all she could hear was the tick of the clock and the sudden soar of birdsong in the quiet country road.

'Davina, is that why you were so frightened to come home?' He turned to look at her.

'No. I didn't know about this till last night. I guessed he hadn't believed me about Philip, that time . . . two years ago. But I had no idea he'd become so bitter and . . . twisted about me.'

'Now I understand why you look so awful,' he said quietly.

Not all of it, she thought wryly. She made an effort to pull herself together and think coherently. 'Davina,' he said, not looking at her, 'is there anything else . . . I mean, are there going to be any more surprises coming our way this week-end?'

'No.'

'That means you've seen Philip,' he said flatly as he started the car.

'Yes.'

'All right, let's go.'

Half an hour later they were sitting comfortably in the lounge of the luxurious Cornish Castle where Jake was staying the night. He had ordered coffee, toast and cognac which he insisted Davina eat and drink. After a while she began to feel more normal and tried to talk to him.

'I would like to say something about what happened at home . . .' she began hesitantly.

'When you're feeling stronger, Davina,' he interrupted curtly. 'You'll need all your energy to get through the rest of the day. And I don't think I can take any more emotional upsets. I've had enough for one day.'

His voice was cold, his eyes indifferent as they rested on her face. She looked down at her hands, feeling unexpectedly bereft. She had become used to his support in the last twenty-four hours, his understanding, his attention. Now he was withdrawing from her, she felt suddenly lost and wondered why his coolness should be hurtful.

She looked at him. He was scanning the room, glancing round at other people, and she thought he was probably bored with her, with the wedding. And she couldn't blame him. He was sitting, hands in his pockets, long legs stretched out in front, his height and elegance reducing to insignificance every other man in the room. Davina noticed the envious looks she was getting from women who glanced at him as they passed through, openly admiring, conscious of his magnetism. The profile turned to her was hard and unyielding, the lips tightly compressed, the chin thrust forward and the forehead drawn into a heavy frown.

Had her sister been right about him? Was he the kind of man to make a girl fall in love and become dependent and then leave her to amuse himself elsewhere with other women, even after marriage?

'Please will you listen to me for a moment?' she asked.

Jake sighed impatiently.

'Very well, since you're determined, but make it short, Davina, whatever it is. My patience is wearing a bit thin.'

Undeterred by his brusqueness, she rushed into speech.

'There's no longer any need to go on with this arrangement . . . the engagement, I mean, coming to the wedding and all that. I can manage quite well on my own now, and, as you saw, my father doesn't need protection, as I thought.' He wasn't helping her by looking straight ahead and not saying a word, she thought. 'What I'm trying to say is, if you'd rather go home and not come to the wedding, that's quite all right. I can say your father wasn't well and you were called away . . . you needn't feel obliged to be there because you told my family you would be. They would all understand.' She stopped.

'Have you finished?' he asked tersely.

'Yes.'

'I thought that's what you were bursting to tell me, and I didn't want to discuss it, but since you've forced it on me, there's something that I should have said to you earlier.' He did not look at her. 'You may have noticed during our working partnership that I live to please myself. I don't undertake commitments that I don't want to have, nor do I promise to do things I don't want to do. When I said I wanted this arrangement, I had my reasons, and those still hold. If I'd wanted to get out of coming with you, I could have made any number of opportunities to do so. Am I making myself clear?' His voice was crisp and impatient.

He turned to look at her, and she nodded, her eyes veiled, a mist of tears behind her lashes which she wouldn't let him see.

'My father is expecting us for lunch tomorrow and you're coming to that with me. If you don't want to stay at your home tonight, I can arrange a room for you here at the hotel, and you can bring your things when you come to dinner this evening.'

'No, thank you,' she didn't want him organising anything else for her, 'I'll stay at home for tonight. Mother would be most unhappy if I stopped here, and it would make my father think he'd been right about. . . .'

Jake stiffened as she broke off in confusion.

'Our having an affair, you mean? That's hardly likely,' Jake said cuttingly, 'but I assure you, my dear, if I wanted to have an affair with you I wouldn't allow your father's feelings to stop me.' He stood up. 'Now we'd better get on with the rest of the day.'

CHAPTER SIX

THE Cornish Bay Hotel was ideally suited to wedding receptions. The gold, high-ceilinged room, with its huge french windows to the gardens and trout lake beyond, was impeccably laid out for the event. Along the walls long white-covered tables were ranged, weighed down with flower arrangements, glasses lined up in military precision, flanked by buckets cooling the champagne. Varieties of snacks, canapés and tiny sandwiches were arranged artistically around the room, while in the centre stood the square white three-tiered wedding cake, each level held up by four scrolled columns in traditional style.

Davina could see her parents welcoming the last of the guests by the open door. Monica and Philip, arm in arm, were watching the bridesmaids arranging the last of the wedding presents ready to be photographed. Looking at Philip in morning dress, tall, blond and handsome, she turned away, her mind going back to the church ceremony.

'Bride or groom?' Davina had not recognised the usher who whispered to them as they entered the cool church, almost the last to arrive.

'Bride.' It was Jake who answered, and they walked down the long expanse of carpet to find their seats.

Davina looked up at the stained glass windows high above the altar, and nostalgia hit her for all the days of her childhood which were so definitely gone and past. Life had been so easy then, so uncomplicated.

The organ music seemed almost too much sound for the tiny church, bursting into the aisles with village friends in their festive best, and a few of the groom's more sophisticated London relations. There were flowers everywhere in huge white urns on high pedestals and in banks of small spring blossoms ranged before the altar.

Jake handed her the order of service, and she turned to stare at him slightly bemused to see him standing there, unable to focus for a moment and recall why he was with her. And then the organ swept into the wedding music. Philip appeared with his best man to stand in front of the altar, slightly turned to watch Monica as the bridal procession came up the aisle. Davina too watched her sister, lovely in ivory satin with a train that swept the floor and a long lace veil billowing out around her.

The vicar began the ceremony and Philip and Monica turned their backs to the congregation. As they took their vows Davina swayed and feared she might faint, but Jake pushed her down to sit with her head between her knees till it passed. And then it was all over, and they were out in the lukewarm sunshine, the photographer busy posing the family, darting in and out of bushes and gravestones to snap the best angles. Davina fixed a firm, determined smile on her face and kept it there.

'Champagne.' Jake was beside her, holding a glass with the sparkling liquid.

'Thank you.' She sipped the ice cold bubbly wine, but it made her feel slightly queasy and she merely held on to the glass as though it was a lifeline, giving her something to do with her hands. She looked at Jake, towering above most of the men in the room, looking masculine, sure of himself as always. His face was grim and cold, his mouth set, curling slightly. She knew that expression only too well; it meant things were not to his liking. She thought suddenly how silly that sounded, as though they were both in the office, and she was wondering what had displeased him.

And then suddenly they were the centre of a stream of people brought over by her mother. She was introduced to Philip's parents and friends, greeting his sister with an embarrassed half smile. And they were inundated with a stream of aunts and her mother's friends, all anxious to admire—her ring, her clothes, her obvious, cool self-confidence and, above all, her fiancé. The man she had captured for herself.

And suddenly Davina was fiercely glad to be there with Jake, grateful for his presence. And he was magnificent. He held her hand, impressed and charmed them all, as they took in his height, his good looks, his obvious charm, wealth and success. Even arch questions about wedding dates did not halt him in his stride. He simply looked down at her lovingly and kissed her gently on the cheek, at which she blushed furiously. They were a tremendous hit, until finally he made their excuses and took her away, murmuring something about fresh air and marching her firmly out to the lift and up to his suite.

As he poured himself a whisky Davina sank down on a chair and noted the impersonal quality of the thick pile carpeting, the heavy brocade curtains and soft deep couches. Only a few of his personal things scattered about gave the room any character.

'Here, try this,' he said, holding out a steaming cup of coffee.

'Oh, how wonderful!' she said thankfully.

The hot sweet liquid cleared her head and she sat back, leaning thankfully against the cushions.

'Can we leave now, do you think?' she asked, eyes closed.

'Not yet. You'll have to wait for the speeches and the cake cutting.' His voice was impersonal again.

She opened her eyes to look at him. He was at the other side of the room, but she could see the lines of strain in his face. He looked pale as though he had not slept well, and she wondered if he was worried about his father. She had seen him worn out at work many times, but not in this grim, forbidding, controlled way. Was he angry with her?

He turned away and walked to the window. 'Well,' he said evenly, 'you saw Philip last night, I gather. Was everything sorted out between you?'

Davina didn't answer.

Jake moved from the window and came towards her. 'Well?' he repeated insistently.

'I don't believe our arrangement included lengthy confidences . . . on either side,' she said shortly, fully aware she sounded rather petulant and childish.

'I see,' his voice grated harshly. 'You gave me your confidence in London, and now we're suddenly strangers, and I'm to be told nothing. Perhaps you feel I have no right? Let me assure you I have every right. If you and Philip have been making love while you're supposed to be engaged to me, it becomes very much my business. Perhaps you were seen?'

Davina gasped. Had they been seen last night on the beach? Could Jake have been there? She looked up at him, her eyes wide and her mouth trembling. Her throat felt constricted, and she didn't know what to say.

'I did see him,' she brought out at last.

'Alone?' he rapped out at her.

'Yes, alone,' she snapped, suddenly angry, 'and it's none of your business. Whatever you say, our engagement is only a farce.'

'I suppose you told your precious Philip that too?' His mouth curled with a sneer.

'No, I didn't!' her voice was trembling. 'How could I? I had to explain why I wouldn't run away with him.'

Jake expelled a sigh as though he had been holding his breath. 'You did make that clear to him, then?'

'Yes, of course. He was to marry my sister today, wasn't he? What else could I do?'

'Does that mean you found out you don't love him any more?'

She said nothing.

Her silence seemed to infuriate him. He strode to the window and back again, hands pushed deep into his trouser pockets. At last he stopped.

'Davina, when are you going to wake up? Your Philip is just as much a dreamer as you. He doesn't love you. He doesn't love anyone but himself. And how long do you think that would make you happy?'

'How do you know what he's like?' she snapped. 'You met him once for a few minutes and yet you know all about him. You don't know him at all . . .' her voice broke and she stopped.

'Do you think he would look after you, stay faithful to you, make a home for you and your children?' Jake was controlling his anger with difficulty. 'Isn't it time you came out of the clouds where your emotions have been clamped for the last two years, and found what life is really like? What emotions are all about?'

'How dare you talk to me like that!' she exclaimed, her anger rising, her breasts heaving. 'You don't know anything about me or what I feel. Just because I don't play around getting experience like your lady friends. . . .' She stopped, aghast at what she had said.

Jake stopped walking and stood still. 'Is that what you think I mean?' His voice was very quiet.

'Yes . . . no . . . . how should I know what you mean?' She was near to tears.

He turned his back on her. 'I'm talking about feelings, not dreams.' His voice was harsh again with urgency, some kind of suppressed emotion. 'You've been living in a dream, Davina, with your absent Philip. Dreams are safe and don't hurt, but they're also lifeless and cold.'

She said nothing, her face rigid with tension and fear at his tone. He seemed to be whipping himself into some kind of fury, and she didn't know what to do. He turned to her, his head back, lids lowered over his eyes, his lips curled contemptuously.

'Life is just too difficult for you, isn't it? It's all so confusing,' he drawled.

Davina got up. 'I'm going back downstairs,' she said, wanting only to get away.

'Just one moment,' he said coldly, and moved towards her.

'No,' she said, 'I don't want to go on with this . . . please!'

He ignored her.

'Perhaps the time has come to bring you down out of those clouds and dispel some of that confusion.' He took her by the shoulders, and for a moment surprise kept her motionless. She looked up into his face with a sudden premonition.

'No!' She twisted in his hold. 'No, Jake, please!' Her voice was panic-stricken. 'Please don't, Jake!'

Ignoring her efforts to be free, he put his arms round her, enveloping her completely, crushing her body with his own and imprisoning her hands against his chest. He looked into her frightened eyes, and bent his head, fastening his mouth to her lips in a hard, brutal kiss which rocked her against him, her head forced back on her neck by the pressure of his lips.

She tried to pull away, to free her mouth from his, but his grip tightened painfully, and his kiss hardened as he parted her lips with his. She could feel the heat of his body and the taut muscles straining her closer, anger in his hold. She felt completely helpless and suddenly stopped fighting him. As her resistance to him drained away, the anger seemed to leave him. He lifted his head, and his fierce hold on her eased. He moved his lips slowly and sensually against her mouth, and she quivered in his arms, suddenly awakened to a response she had never felt before. Her senses flamed at his touch, and she returned his kiss with fire and passion, her mind whirling out of control. Jake lifted a hand to cradle her head and she wound her arms round his neck, her fingers caressing the thick, crisp hair as his kiss deepened demandingly, and his hold on her tightened.

And then suddenly she was free. He put her away from him slowly and deliberately. They were both breathing raggedly, and he turned his back and walked away. Davina's legs felt as though they would collapse under her, and she reached behind for the sofa, sinking thankfully into its depth, trying to recover her composure.

Jake poured himself a large whisky and drank it straight down.

Her lips felt tender, and she was trembling uncontrollably, her face aflame with colour.

The silence seemed endless. Then he turned to her, his face expressionless, his head back and eyes veiled by thick dark lashes against the unexpected whiteness of his face.

'My apologies,' he drawled. 'That . . . got a little out of hand.'

She looked away from him, tensing at the tone in his voice. She was afraid she might be sick, and sat quite still.

'Davina,' his voice was suddenly sharply anxious, 'are you all right?' He put down his glass and started towards her.

'Please——' she began, when suddenly the phone shrilled and she jumped at the unexpected noise.

Jake picked up the receiver.

'Yes,' he began. 'No, around noon, if that's all right. . . .'

Davina got up quietly, walked unsteadily to the door behind Jake's back, and made her way out into the corridor.

In a slight daze she found a ladies' room which was blessedly empty, and sat down on a stool in front of the mirrors, staring horrified at her own reflection. Her eyes were huge and dark in her pale, strained face, her hair dislodged from its neat coil, and her make-up hopelessly smudged. She pulled herself together and set about methodically repairing the damage. After a wash she felt better, and by the time she had arranged her hair and used her perfume spray, a touch of lipstick made her feel almost back to normal, ready to go downstairs.

She was tempted to run out on everything and everyone, take the next train back to London, but she put that idea out of her mind. It wasn't possible.

She clamped down completely on what had just happened with Jake. She didn't want to think about it, to remember it. Later, she told herself firmly, but not right away.

Jake was pacing the foyer as she came out of the lift on the ground floor. He stopped and looked at her intently for a moment, before he took her lightly by the elbow and they returned to the reception.

The toasts and speeches were under way and the cake cutting followed. Finally Monica stood on the hotel stairs and threw down her bouquet straight at Davina, who dropped it as though it burnt her, and everyone laughed gaily.

It was beginning to darken into dusk as Jake drove her home. On the doorstep he stopped for a moment as though about to speak. She looked up at him fearfully in the half dark.

'Thank you,' she said in a polite little voice.

'I'll pick you up at eight,' he said brusquely. 'Try and get some rest.'

Davina let herself into the empty house, relieved to be alone at last. As she heard the Rolls drive away she ran upstairs, took off her clothes and climbed into bed.

Once more she was awakened by a loud knocking on the door.

'Ina, wake up, it's late!' It was her mother's voice.

'Yes, Mum, I'm awake. Hang on a second, I'm coming.'

She jumped out of bed and flung on a dressing gown. Her mother was at the door in a housecoat.

'Hello,' Davina said sleepily. 'I must have dropped off. Come in.'

Mrs Richards looked at her daughter's face steadily for a moment and then turned away. 'I was just getting us a cup of tea and wondered if you'd like one. We're having it in the kitchen, but I can bring you one up here if you prefer?' She sounded almost embarrassed as she hesitated. 'You don't look so good. Would you rather give it a miss tonight?' she asked anxiously. 'Perhaps it's all been a bit much.'

'What?' Davina was puzzled. 'No, I'm fine. I was a bit tired—I didn't sleep too well last night, but I must go. Whatever would Monica and ... everyone think if I didn't turn up?' she ended lamely.

'Very well, dear, whatever you say.' Her mother turned back. 'Why don't you have a nice refreshing shower first and then come down? I'll make a fresh pot.'

She closed the door, and Davina turned back into the room, catching sight of herself in the mirror. Her eyes widened in horror. She looked ghastly. Her lips were swollen and vividly bruised, her eyes darkly shadowed and there was a terrible purple bruise on her arm. No wonder her mother had stared! But there was no time for thinking and dreaming, she reflected wryly, and stripped off. Within moments she was under the shower. Then, wrapped in a voluminous towelling coat, she wandered down to the kitchen.

Her father was sitting at the kitchen table, dressed in comfortable old tweeds, and reading the paper. 'Ah, there you are, dear,' her mother said. 'Come and sit down.'

For a moment Davina wanted to run again, but she controlled herself and sat down opposite him. He looked up briefly and acknowledged her with a nod.

Her mother glanced at her and smiled with relief. Davina grinned back uneasily as she helped herself to tea.

'Lovely,' she said. 'Just what I need.'

There was a pause.

'Well,' Davina said cheerfully, 'that all went off very successfully, didn't it?'

'Yes,' her father said coolly, 'it was very well planned.'

'Is Jake coming to pick you up, love?' her mother asked.

'Yes, about eight.'

'Well, you'd better hurry with that tea. It's nearly that now.'

Her father got up. 'Well, I must go and do some work, so I'll leave you two to gossip.'

'Work?' Her mother's voice was astounded. 'Why, whatever do you mean? We agreed to have a nice quiet evening in front of the telly. What work?'

'I ... er ... I've some letters to do,' he said rather stiffly, picked up his paper and his cup and went off.

Davina clenched her hands round her cup.

'That's odd,' her mother said reflectively. 'He seemed so much more relaxed. We had a long talk when we got home and I thought. . . .' She went over to the sink.

'Never mind,' Davina said, 'he's probably not in the mood for company.'

'Mm. . . .' her mother said thoughtfully.

With her father's going the atmosphere changed, and Davina longed suddenly to confide in her mother, tell her the truth about Jake, the engagement and everything. But she remained silent. She couldn't do it. And once started no one knew there such confidences would end. Anyway, she was leaving in the morning.

'I think you father is coming round, don't you, love?' her mother asked anxiously.

'Mm, maybe.' Davina wasn't so sure.

Mrs Richards sighed. 'I hope so. And now,' she said more cheerfully, 'tell me what you're going to wear tonight.'

Twenty minutes later Davina looked at herself in the mirror and decided that the silk chiffon dress was well worth the time and money she had spent on it. Soft folds fell from narrow shoulder straps showing her creamy skin, to a tightly belted waistband. The pale lilac brought out the chestnut tints in her freshly washed hair, and she liked the feel of the full skirt billowing round her, the pale pink underskirt revealed through side slits as she walked.

Her make-up was heavier than usual, but she hoped no one would notice in the subdued lights of the hotel restaurant. Her lips she had rouged heavily and glossed to hide the bruises, and her blusher had needed much more application than she would normally use.

The doorbell rang downstairs, and she picked up her black fur jacket, her purse and, with a last glance in the mirror, made her way downstairs.

Jake was chatting to her mother in the hall and she had a good look at him on her way down. She had never seen him in evening dress, and recognised how well it suited his dark looks. Black dinner jacket and the gleam of frilled white shirt with bow tie emphasised the breadth of his shoulders and the darkness of his hair and skin. As she approached them, she noticed he looked even more remote and cool than he had done when he left her earlier in the evening.

'Darling you look lovely!' It was her mother's voice,

and Jake turned to acknowledge her with a slight nod and a smile which did not reach his eyes.

'Thank you, Mum.' Davina leaned forward and kissed her mother gently on the cheek.

'There, you mustn't spoil your make-up,' said Mrs Richards, giving her daughter a little hug. 'I think we must be going,' said Jake. 'We're rather late.'

He turned to her mother and bowed slightly. Davina recognised the gesture as one he adopted when he was bored or anxious to be gone. She looked round the hall, but there was no sign of her father. With a quick nervous look at her mother, she followed Jake out.

It was a dark clear night and neighbouring houses were shuttered in for the evening. The silence lasted till they were seated in the car and Jake turned it towards St Ives.

Davina started, 'I think. . . .'

'Save it, Davina,' he interrupted her coolly. 'If you're going to go on about obligations at me tonight I might hit ou and regret it. Just don't talk.'

She bit her lip and sat stiffly at his side, her eyes fixed on the movement of the headlights flickering on the road ahead. After a while she felt a little silly. Easing herself into a more comfortable position, she watched him from under her lashes. In the light from the dashboard she could see his hands clearly, holding the wheel lightly, but with power held in reserve. They were broad and strong—how strong she had discovered that afternoon. The nails were spatulate and beautifully kept, and faint dark hairs grew lightly towards the wrist where his gold watch gleamed in the half dark.

She could smell his aftershave lotion and also that tang that was solely him and very masculine. Her eyes travelled to his face where the mouth was now lightly set, showing the firm moulding of the lips, the lower slightly fuller, revealing in repose the latent sensuality of the mouth. He did not move under her scrutiny, his eyes intent on the road.

Something moved and twisted painfully inside her. Her

throat constricted, and she had a slight premonition of danger; that something quite dreadful was going to happen to her world.

It was Saturday night and the hotel restaurant was crowded for the popular weekly dinner-dance. Jake and Davina made a handsome couple, standing side by side in the entrance looking for their party, and more than one head turned as they made their way across the room to the wedding table.

'Darlings!' It was Monica hailing them. 'You're late.' She gestured to the place beside her on the plush sofa. 'Come and sit here next to me, brother-in-law to be. Davina, love, you sit next to Harry. I promised him,' she said vaguely.

Jake bowed to Monica, carrying her hand to his lips and complimenting her on her looks.

Sitting down, Davina recognised her table partner as the usher at the church, and gave him a dazzling smile. 'Hello,' she said.

'A drink?' he asked her, slightly bemused.

'Thank you,' she said. 'A dry Martini, please.'

It was the first time Davina had dined at the Cornish Castle and she looked round with interest. High-ceilinged as the room she had seen earlier in the day, it was lit by huge crystal chandeliers that tinkled in the breeze generated by old-fashioned fans rotating slowly. The tables, covered with pale pink damask, reflected the dusky pink of heavy velvet curtains at the high windows, and the deep rose of the thick carpet underfoot. All round she noted elegantly gowned and jewelled diners, faces gleaming in the light of tall pink candles set on every table in huge glass bowls. The orchestra in evening dress was playing on a raised platform above the dance floor, which was already crowded.

'Dance, Davina?' Jake's voice was a question, but he expected no refusal, as he pulled back her chair. On the dance floor she moved quite naturally into his arms. In her high heels she reached almost to his chin and she could feel his breath against her hair, and the hardness of his legs against hers as they moved and he held her tightly to him. He took her hand and placed the palm down inside his open jacket. She could feel the crisp dark hair through the thin material, and curled her fingers, rubbing them gently against him. He pulled her closer and put his lips to her temple, caressing her skin.

Davina was bemused, trembling slightly at his nearness, but feeling strangely safe and protected in his arms. Her own pulses were hammering and she was responding to his touch as she had done earlier in the day.

She tipped her head back and surprised a look of some strong emotion in his eyes, keeping his face still and intent as he searched her eyes rather blindly for a moment, before he pulled her head back against him and looked away.

She was shaken by that look and the effect it had on her. What was this yearning for closeness, this wanting she didn't recognise? Was it some kind of infatuation? She hoped not. A man like Jake was out of her class. She hadn't the experience or the expertise to cope with him. Having an affair with Jake could only spell disaster, because there was just one way it would end. He always moved on, whatever the lady in question might feel or want. Oh, dear, no!

'May I?' It was Philip cutting in on them.

Davina said nothing, but waited for the men to sort it out.

'Sorry,' Jake's voice was cold and cutting, 'we were just going for something to eat.'

'I won't keep her for long.' Philip was coaxing, looking down at her. 'Just once around the floor.' He turned to Jake. 'You won't object, will you? After all, old man,' he gave a short rather strident laugh, 'you'll have her for the rest of her life, won't you? You can't grudge me one dance?'

'Davina?' Jake's eyes were on her face.

'I'll follow you in a moment, Jake,' she said lightly, not looking at him.

Jake took his arms away immediately and left them.

Davina shivered suddenly at his going, and Philip pulled her into his arms and they began to dance.

'I thought I'd never get a single word with you today. He's been guarding you like a bloodhound.' He pulled her closer 'Have you missed me?' he breathed, his mouth against her face.

'Please, Philip! You're married now. Do stop flirting with me.' She pulled herself slightly away from him, wondering why she didn't feel weak at the knees as she usually did when he held her.

'Flirting? Is that what you think I'm doing?' Philip's voice was hurt.

'I'm sorry, Philip, but I really don't want this kind of conversation with you any more. You're married to my sister now, and as far as I'm concerned, that means you're my brother-in-law. Nothing more.'

'My, my, you do sound prudish all of a sudden! That's not how you reacted last night on the beach, is it, my love? Do you honestly think I don't know how you feel about me? I know you still love me as much as you always did. I can feel it—I felt it last night when you kissed me.'

'No, Philip, you're wrong.' She was getting impatient with him. 'Last night I suppose I was surprised to see you, a bit nostalgic, I expect. But that's all.'

'I don't believe you.' He sounded almost smug. 'Oh, I know you're supposed to be engaged, but that won't last long.'

'What do you mean?' she demanded.

'Well, it's obvious he's not your style—he's much too old for you and too sophisticated. He'll be forever globe-trotting and amusing himself while you stay at home having babies. I imagine you turned to him on the rebound, especially as you work for him. They do say all secretaries fall in love with their bosses. But they don't marry them. Once he's on to the next lovely, you'll wake up and find out what he's really like.'

Davina was furious, not least because she had been thinking much the same things herself only moments earlier. But that didn't give Philip the right to say them.

'How dare you talk like that about Jake? I'm sorry, Philip, but I won't listen to that kind of talk about my ... er ... fiancé.' Her voice was quiet and curiously firm, and he looked down at her in surprise.

'You really have a crush on him, then?' he said. 'That explains the ring. Well, dear, you can take it from me, you're out of your depth. Forget it and forget him. I daresay he finds you a novelty, but it won't last.'

Davina was speechless as a strange pain hit her at his words. Philip did know her pretty well, after all. Perhaps he could see the situation more clearly than she could. And perhaps he was right.

She sighed. It really made no difference to anything. She had known it herself anyway; it just hurt her pride to have it put into words by someone else.

'No, my darling,' Philip was saying, whispering to her intimately, 'you stick with me. We can meet in London and see each other. I'll teach you what real love is like, because I adore you. For me there's no one else and there never will be.'

'Philip, you're being ridiculous! You don't seriously imagine you and I will be meeting secretly when you're married to my sister? What do you take me for?' She was angry now. 'Please take me back to the table.'

'Darling, I didn't mean to. . . .'

'Now, Philip,' she said, adamant, and stopped still on the dance floor, stepping out of his arms.

He looked furious for a moment and then took her hand and walked off the floor with her. Davina removed her hand firmly from his and went ahead.

As they sat down, the men at the table rose politely and she looked up to find Jake's eyes on her, his face set in anger. Her face paled and she clenched her hands to compose herself.

'Your soup will be cold.' Jake's voice reached her, cool and distant. 'Shall I order some more?'

'No, thank you,' she said politely, looking away from him.

'Ina love,' it was Monica, 'come and freshen up with

me in the powder room, will you?'

They wended their way through the tables, admiring glances following. They made a stunningly contrasting pair. In the ladies' room Monica turned to her sister. 'I wanted to talk to you, and this evening seems to be the only time left.' She spoke quietly.

She was wearing a low-necked blue satin dress, tight-waisted with a full, stiff skirt, and it showed up the dark hair and the pale skin of arms and shoulders. Davina thought she had never seen Monica look so lovely, so blooming.

'That's a lovely dress, Monica. It suits you beautifully,' she said, wondering apprehensively what her sister wanted to discuss.

'Thank you.' Monica seemed nervous too as she sought to find the right words. 'I want to tell you how sorry I am about today . . . the things I said. I was . . . er . . . frightened, terrified, that well, that you and Philip might . . . that he might persuade you to run away with him at the last moment.' She stopped awkwardly, and Davina wanted to give her some kind reassurance, but couldn't think of the right way to do it. 'I know, of course, that he has a thing about you,' Monica went on, 'but I've felt for a time now that he really does love me, although he wouldn't admit it, of course. If I thought he didn't love me I wouldn't have married him today and I certainly wouldn't be having his child.' She paused, but didn't look at her sister. 'You see, he's weak in some ways . . . about money, about other women. He's easily flattered because he's vain.' She looked rather anxiously across at Davina, who didn't move or respond. She sighed and went on tentatively,

'Well, I understand about these things and he knows I don't take them too seriously. I love him and I'm weak in other things . . . where I need him. But he has this dream about you. You're the golden girl he never had, but thinks he always wants, always loves. Only it's not real. It's a dream he can retreat into when he feels a failure or he's getting older or when something goes wrong. Do you understand what I'm getting at?'

Davina didn't say anything.

'Davina, please, I don't want to go on if I'm hurting you . . . please help me! I'm fighting—not for Philip, I've got him now. I'm fighting for us. I . . . I want us to be sisters again, somehow.'

Davina found tears pricking her eyelids and kept her eyes closed.

'Go on,' she whispered, 'please. I'm listening.'

'When you came yesterday and you and Philip saw each other last night, secretly, alone. . . .'

'Quite unexpectedly,' Davina interrupted. 'It wasn't planned.'

'Maybe not. I think Philip did plan it. Anyway, when you came and looked so radiantly beautiful, I was suddenly not sure—not sure of Philip, not sure if I was right about his feelings about you. And I felt Jake wasn't quite for real. Oh, I know it sounds silly, but I almost felt it was all arranged, that you'd become engaged on the rebound or just because of the wedding. I didn't feel you two were in love at all. It felt almost as though you were strangers to each other. It was all a bit confused. But I was scared, and that's why I said those awful things this morning . . . about you and Jake.'

She stopped, and still Davina said nothing.

'Will you forgive me?' Monica was close to tears. 'I realise now how wrong I was. Watching you at the reception and again tonight, I can't imagine how I ever thought you weren't in love. It's written all over you both. He can't keep his eyes off you, and you obviously adore him. And I feel very silly and stupid, and so guilty still about . . . that other hurt, two years ago. I can't ever forget . . . it still haunts me.'

'I'm glad you mentioned that,' at last Davina spoke. 'I've often thought I lost two people that day, not just Philip, but you. It would be nice if somehow we could find a way back to each other.'

And suddenly Monica had her arms round her younger sister and was hugging her tightly. 'You are happy, aren't you, Davina!' her voice was anxious.

Davina smiled, eyes veiled. 'What do you think?' she said, and turned away to the mirror, using a tissue on her eyes. She knew they would never return to the easy, confident closeness of childhood, but she was glad that something could be rescued of their relationship, that they would not continue as enemies.

But there were things now she would have to hide from her sister. There was no way Monica must be allowed to guess how close she had been to the truth about Jake and herself, about their engagement.

'Do you remember,' Monica said dreamily, 'how we used to have long talks about love and marriage? How we would wait for the real thing, never compromise, never give ourselves out of curiosity?' She wiped her eyes regarding her face in the mirror, not looking at her sister. 'How long ago that seems, doesn't it?'

Davina straightened. 'The men are going to wonder how long ago it seems since they saw us if we don't get back to the table,' she said brightly. 'They'll probably think we've been kidnapped!'

It was the last dance and Davina was exhausted. She had danced gaily with everyone all evening, everyone except Jake, who had not asked her again. He had taken each girl in rotation on to the dance floor, smiling, joking and charming them, until she had followed him several times with her eyes, wondering at her own sense of depression at his neglect. And now he was at her side.

'Come along,' he said almost curtly, and she got up. On the dance floor he pulled her close into his arms, pushing her head against his shoulder and placing her arms round his waist under his open jacket. The lights dimmed till only the flicker of guttering candles lit the remote corners of the room. They moved slowly to the dreamy waltz, their arms round each other. Couples were kissing unashamedly all round them.

Davina felt Jake's lips against her cheek, moving to her mouth, and she lifted her head for his kiss. He kissed her deeply and the heat spread through her as desire for him raced through her body. She kissed him back, her arms tightening round him, and his mouth hardened possessively, passionate and demanding. They stood still, bodies locked together, lost to their surroundings, until suddenly the music stopped and the lights went up. Jake took his lips away unhurriedly and held her head against him for a moment, giving her time to recover. Then, holding her closely to his side, he took her back to the table, relinquishing her hand reluctantly as she sat down.

The clock on the dashboard showed nearly two o'clock as he drove her home. Neither spoke. Davina leaned back, eyes closed. She felt drained. Too much had happened in one day. She couldn't feel any more.

The streets were empty and the powerful car took only minutes to cover the distance. As Jake stopped the car outside her house, she opened her eyes and looked at him. He did not switch off the lights nor the engine. She didn't move, half expecting him to reach for her, to kiss her again, and she knew she wanted him to do just that.

'Do you mind if I don't see you to the door?' he said indifferently. 'I'd like to turn straight round.'

'Of course not.' She had the door open and was out in one movement, failing to notice his hands clenching on the wheel till his knuckles whitened.

'I'll pick you up in the morning about eleven-thirty,' he said, '. . . this morning.'

'Fine,' she said quietly, and sped through the gate to the front door.

Before she had the key in the door, he had turned the car, the beam of headlights travelling across her briefly before he disappeared round the corner.

CHAPTER SEVEN

DAVINA woke in the morning as the bright sunlight touched her face. The open, uncurtained windows showed her a warm spring sky, and she looked at her watch. Great heavens, it was half past ten!

She jumped out of bed, feeling refreshed and ready for the day ahead. Showered and powdered, she chose one of her favourite fine cord suits, a moss green, with a pale pink angora sweater and darker green suede shoes.

She was not sure if her parents were up and made her way quietly down to the kitchen.

'Good morning, my love.' Her mother was dressed and cooking, and had obviously been up for hours. She sounded gay and, after a long and searching look at her daughter's more relaxed face, she went on with bacon and toast. 'I heard you move and thought you might like a cooked breakfast this morning.'

'Mm . . . yes, lovely. I'm starving, Mum, and I'll have the lot, whatever you're making.'

'Good. I waited for you, so we can have it together. I gather it was a big success last night,' her mother went on. 'Monica rang before they flew off this morning and she sounded happy and contented.'

'Yes,' Davina's voice was guarded and casual, 'it was all beautifully done—food, the band, everything.' She looked round. 'Where's Dad?'

'Oh, he's gone out with Jake.'

'What?' Davina shrieked.

'Davina, don't scream at me like that. Whatever . . .' Their eyes met. 'Yes, well, all right. I was a bit surprised myself, but Jake rang earlier to find out how you were, and your father took the call. They arranged to meet and Dad has taken him for a drink at the golf club.'

'Oh, Mum,' Davina sounded worried, 'I do hope that's

all it is, and there's not going to be more trouble. I don't want Jake to be . . .' Her voice tailed off.

'I know, dear. I felt the same, and I tackled your father with it before he went. But he was quite adamant. He was only going to apologise to Jake about . . . well, about yesterday.'

'Well, I hope he sticks to that and doesn't make more mischief,' sighed Davina.

'I know what you must be feeling, but I'm sure it'll be all right,' said her mother reassuringly.

'I doubt if you know what I'm feeling,' Davina said drily, tucking into her scrambled eggs. 'How long have they been gone?' she added casually.

Her mother looked at the clock. 'Oh, about half an hour,' she said. 'Dad insisted they wouldn't be long.'

'I'd better go and pack my things, then.' Davina got up. 'That was delicious, Mum. Do you want me to strip the bed or shall I leave it?'

'Just leave everything. I've plenty of time now to see to it all.' Mrs Richards paused for a moment. 'I suppose we'll not be seeing you again now,' she said, anxious suddenly.

Davina turned back at the door. 'Whatever made you think that?'

'Well, your father thought after yesterday . . . the scene with Jake . . . that you wouldn't want to come back,' her mother said unhappily.

'What nonsense,' Davina said cheerfully. 'I'll be back for a weekend as soon as I can get away.' She stopped and hesitated. 'Of course, Jake won't always have the time to come with me, but you won't mind seeing me alone, will you?' She looked at the clock. 'I must go now.'

'Ina,' her mother's voice stopped her again, 'have you . . . talked to your father at all?'

'No . . . there really hasn't been the time.' Davina looked at her mother's anxious face. 'And we're due at Jake's father's.' She went back and kissed her mother gently. 'Don't worry, Mum, it's all going to be all right. It'll just take time.'

'Perhaps you're right, but I have a feeling, now that Monica is happily settled, it will be easier. He'll have more time to see the whole thing in perspective.' Mrs Richards patted her daughter's cheek. 'Yesterday I was very worried, I must admit. You looked so . . . shattered, somehow. But I can see it's all right again. Now go and get your things together before the men get back.'

The moment Davina saw Jake, she knew something was very wrong. When the two men returned, he was in a black mood, taciturn, grim and forbidding. While they were saying their goodbyes to her parents, he managed to smile and appear cheerful, but she knew him too well to be deceived. As soon as they had left the village he stopped pretending.

She tried to break the silence.

'Jake, will you tell me something about your family before we get there? About your life, things that I should know?'

'Oh, Davina, for heaven's sake, what for? You'll see it all when you get there and anything you don't know, you can ask me. Why should I start on a potted autobiography now? Leave it alone, there's a good girl.'

Half an hour later she tried again.

'Did you discuss . . . I mean, when you were out with my father, did he say anything about . . . was he rude to you again, did he upset you?'

'He was not offensive, Davina, and I'm not upset. What makes you think anything to do with your family would upset me?' he drawled slowly. He paused for a moment. 'Look, Davina,' he went on, 'this week-end is nearly over. The worst is finished for you. So we've only my father to worry about now. Then I plan to get into the car and back to London as quickly as possible.'

Davina bit her lip and said no more. He was right, she was behaving like a silly schoolgirl. Why should she worry what he might be feeling? After all, this whole thing was his idea, not hers. If it had backfired on him—well, he had only himself to blame. She was not in the business of making things easier for him. He could keep his arrogance to himself from now on, she decided.

She leaned back and closed her eyes. How very different this journey was from the one they had shared two days earlier. It seemed a lifetime ago that they had talked naturally, easily with no constraint between them.

She had never been infatuated before. Was this what it felt like? All this fire and flame and desire to the point of wantonness? She wished she knew. She certainly wanted Jake, and wondered what it would be like to have an affair with him. Could she do it? Could she give herself to someone just for a while, until he got fed up or met someone more desirable? She knew plenty of girls who managed it and enjoyed it. Why then did it seem so impossible for her? Monica was right: she didn't think she could do it. Perhaps when they got back to London, all this would drop away. Maybe it was only the enforced intimacy they had shared that brought on all this heady emotion? That and Jake's expertise and experience. After all, he was expert at making love. With her complete lack of any proper experience she was bound to succumb to his attentions. It obviously meant nothing to him at all. He'd probably forgotten all about their lovemaking.

Perhaps they could return to their safe, comfortable, secretary-boss relationship when they got back to London. The more Davina thought about it, the more she felt it to be the answer. They would both forget all about this weekend. After all, they had been putting on a performance; Jake had said that himself . . . a performance for others. That was how the whole thing had started.

'Davina,' Jake was speaking sharply, 'we're nearly there. Are you asleep again? I don't know how you can sleep endlessly the way you do, just dropping off.'

'I'm sorry. No, I wasn't asleep. Just thinking.' She sat up.

'Mm. . . .' He seemed in a better humour, and she glanced at him sideways. His face was certainly more relaxed, but she noticed again his pallor and the dark shadows under his eyes, more so than yesterday. She realised she knew very much less about him than he did about her after this week-end, and wondered if that state of affairs was about to be changed.

As they approached Mevagissey, Jake turned inland and they passed several signposts to villages above the harbour, until he swung off to Portheron. They travelled slowly through the village, past the church, unexpectedly surrounded by palm trees, reminding Davina how warm the climate could be on the Cornish coast. Below her she could see the headland in the distance with its coves and soft sandy beaches at the bottom of steep and rocky cliffs.

The road was now no more than a track, and Jake was slowing right down, until he turned sharply into an open wide gate up a gravelled drive to stop outside a beautiful old stone house set back into bushes of white and purple lilac.

'We're here,' Jake said briefly, and they both got out.

Davina could see a curving lawn to one side of the house, dipping away to what looked like a small lake, while a wood nestled against the other side of the house. She guessed the gardens at the back would face the sea. French windows downstairs gave on to a wide stone terrace running round to the sides of the house with a heavy carved stone balustrade. The Cornish stone of the house was covered to the upper floors in ivy which glistened in the sun and trailed across the balconies of upstairs windows. Suddenly the heavy oak front door opened, and a girl ran out and threw herself at Jake, kissing him passionately on the mouth. For what seemed an endless moment they were locked in each other's arms, and Davina felt a shaft of agonising pain tear through her, keeping her rooted to the spot.

A sudden barking broke the silence as a huge English sheepdog came bounding round the corner of the house, white fur flying, big black ears flopping excitedly, his widely spaced paws covering the distance in no time between himself and his master. He also flung himself at Jake, nearly toppling them both over.

Jake released himself to embrace the dog, but it was the girl who spoke first.

'Oh, Henry,' she sounded rather breathless, 'couldn't you have waited to let me have another minute?'

Jake was scratching the dog's ears, sending him into a blissful ecstasy. 'How are you, wretch?' he asked, and stretched out a hand to Davina. 'Darling, this is Anita Woolland, a neighbour and a pest.' He pulled Davina to his side. 'This is my fiancée, Davina Richards.'

The girl's face was tight with dislike as she dismissed Davina in her smart outfit with obvious disdain.

'Oh, yes,' she said lightly, 'I've heard all about that,' and she linked herself to Jake's other arm, peeping up at him adoringly from under her lashes.

She was lovely, Davina noted. Dark curly hair rioted round a well shaped head, showing up almond skin, large brown eyes and a wide-lipped red mouth. She was wearing skin-tight leather pants and a stretch shirt that barely buttoned across her small pointed breasts. Very curvaceous and tiny, Davina guessed her to be about eighteen years old.

'Where's Dad?' Jake asked her.

'Inside, waiting for you.'

'Are we to be honoured with your company for lunch?'

'I can't,' she wailed, 'there's someone arriving and Daddy wants me to entertain him . . . do you think I'll be able to charm him, Jake?'

'I doubt it,' Jake said cheerfully, and she pouted.

'Oh, you're hateful!' she said mockingly.

'So hateful I was about to suggest a quick ride before lunch. Have you got riding clothes here?' He turned to Davina. 'You won't mind keeping Father company for half an hour, will you, darling?' He bent to kiss her cheek. 'I'm longing for a bit of fresh air.'

'No, of course not.' She knew she was blushing.

'Good. Now all I have to do is to placate Mrs Bateman and persuade her to delay lunch. Come on, imp, in we go,' and he gave Anita's bottom a light slap. She squealed with delight, and ran up the step ahead of him into the front door. Davina was suddenly bored with all the childish exhibitionism.

As they entered the hall she had a brief impression of a light, wood-panelled square entrance with huge black and white tiles covering the floor to the beautiful mahogany stairs leading to the upper floors. She stood still as a man in a wheelchair came through an archway from the back of the house. At the sight of him Davina drew in her breath with a sudden quiver. It was Jake's double.

The impressive height was there, clearly evident even in the wheelchair, the breadth of shoulder, the long legs and the piercing grey eyes. They were all there, even the finely chiselled mouth and the cleft in the centre of the chin. And then the illusion passed as he came forward into the light, and she saw that the hair was quite white, and there were deep lines running from nose to mouth. The eyes, though fiercely bright, were sunken and the cheeks hollow. But the expression was the same. She might have been looking at Jake as he could be, perhaps, one day. It was like a sudden glimpse into the future, and she felt rigid with shock, unable to move at the thought.

She turned to look at Jake behind her, and found him standing motionless, his eyes on her with a terrible dark, bleak pain in them. He seemed to be in the grip of some emotion, some memory that was tearing him apart.

Ignoring everyone, she moved swiftly over to him, took his hand and raised herself on tiptoe to kiss him gently on the cheek. He put an arm round her, gripping her convulsively to him, so that she could hardly breathe. She stood quite still in his arms, until he released her and his look returned to normal and he took her hand, leading her back to his father.

'You must be Davina,' the man in the wheelchair said in Jake's voice. 'My son isn't usually so remiss in his introductions. I am, of course, his father, as you noticed.' His voice was dry with some amusement in it. He held out his hand and she took it warmly in hers, noting the firmness of the grip and the dryness of the palm, hardened from working the chair.

Jake leaned down to kiss his father.

'Sorry we're late, Dad,' and he wheeled the chair round into the living room at the back of the house. It was low-ceilinged with huge dark beams, wide and long, probably running the complete width of the house, Davina guessed. At one end was a large grand piano, low sofas lined the back wall and opposite, the outer wall was made entirely of glass. This was now open to the midday sun which showed up the medley of blues in the room, from walls washed in pale Wedgwood to the tufted blue and primrose carpet and the velvet of upholstery and pale blue linen of the curtains. All round the walls were prints of sailing boats interspersed with family photographs.

Davina stopped in the doorway with an exclamation of delight.

'You like it?' Mr Humphries was pleased. 'Come and sit down, my dear, while Jake pours us all a drink.' He wheeled himself expertly to the side of the sofa.

'Davina?' Jake was at the drinks cabinet.

'Just orange juice, please,' she said rather shyly, aware that Jake's father was looking at her intently.

'Would you mind, Dad, if Nita and I have a quick ride before lunch?'

'If you can persuade Mrs Bateman to hold back lunch,' he replied laughing lightly. He turned to Davina. 'As he'll have told you, Mrs Bateman looks after us and has done since Jake was a little boy. She's supposed to rule us with a rod of iron, but really Jake can wind her round his little finger. Disgraceful, isn't it?' he smiled at his son as Jake brought their drinks.

'O.K., Dad, I'll have a word with her and we'll be off.' He turned to Davina, kissed her lightly on the cheek, leaning down to flick one finger against an errant curl of hair. 'You'll be all right here for a bit?' he asked.

Mr Humphries answered, 'Of course she'll be all right. She's with me, isn't she?'

'Ah, the modesty of the Humphries men,' Jake murmured, and went out. Anita was obviously too restless to stay without Jake and followed him.

Davina wondered if she was following him upstairs and

watching him change. Her hands clenched tightly in her lap as she told herself firmly it was none of her business how Jake ran his private life, either here or in London.

'Now let's be comfortable.' Mr Humphries wheeled his chair round, so that he was looking into her face as she sat against the light. 'Mmm,' he said with a sigh, 'I can see why my errant son fell in love with you. You're quite beautiful.'

Davina blushed. Oh, dear! she thought.

'Ah,' he said, 'and she blushes. That of course is irresistible. I thought they didn't make women who blush any more. I must congratulate my son.'

She looked away from him, wondering what he expected from her in the way of conversation.

'I'm not going to interrogate you, you know. Just have a chat,' he said, twinkling at her. It seemed both Humphries men could read minds. She smiled at him, suddenly quite at ease, and leaned back comfortably.

'It's cosy here,' she said, 'and I certainly envy you your view.'

'Well, I've lived here man and boy, as you might say, for nearly forty years. That's a long time. When my wife died everyone said I should move, that memories would be too much for me. But I didn't, and I'm glad. I would have been miserable anywhere else. And Jake would have lost his home as well as his mother. Instead he grew up here and he loves it as I do ... no, I'm glad I stayed.'

He coughed suddenly and couldn't stop. Davina felt helpless, not knowing what to do. He pointed to his jacket and she put her hand in the pocket to find a bottle. She shook out some pills and he took two as she brought him a glass of water from the drinks cabinet.

He drank and the coughing eased. But it had exhausted him and for a while they sat in silence. Gradually the colour came back into his face and he smiled rather ruefully. 'The penalty of being old,' he said. 'Now, tell me about yourself. I know you have a sister, because I believe she was married yesterday.'

'Yes. It was a lovely wedding and they're away on their

honeymooon, giving my parents a well-earned rest.'

'And now you go back to London?'

She nodded.

'Tell me, have you liked working for my son?'

'It would be more than my job is worth to say no, wouldn't it?' she smiled at him.

'My dear, whatever we discuss here will not be repeated to anyone. I couldn't pump my visitors mercilessly to keep pace with the outside world if they didn't trust to my discretion.'

'Well,' she said simply, 'I love my job. Jake is the kind of boss who somehow gets the best out of us all. There are people at the agency who wouldn't like to work for him. He's exacting, demanding, but expects more from himself than from anyone else—that's probably why we all give him our best. He also gives praise and credit where it's due.'

'That's quite a testimonial. And are you a dedicated career woman? Will you go on working after you're married?'

She should have expected these questions, she supposed, but she was not prepared for them. And she hated lying to this man. She hesitated.

'I'm not really sure what a career woman is,' she said slowly. 'So many so-called career women stop being that when they get married or with their first baby. I don't like the phrase. Whether or not I go on working after . . . marriage . . . is something I haven't yet decided. I would certainly not want to work when the children arrive. I wouldn't want to hand them to someone else to bring up.'

'Well,' he laughed, 'I can't complain I'm not getting answers! Few young women of your age admit to uncertainties and doubts. Let me see, Jake didn't say, but you must be about . . . twenty-one?'

'Almost,' she laughed, 'but I find it's easy to be sure when you're talking about life. It's much harder when you're living it.'

'I would agree with you. But look at young Anita now. She and her family have the stud farm adjoining our land,

and she's been popping in and out of this house since they moved here when she was about twelve years old ... hoping always to find Jake. She's younger than you, but she would never admit to uncertainties about anything. She's always been sure of what she wanted, and it's always been Jake.' He leaned forward. 'You mustn't mind an old man talking. At one time, quite recently in fact, I had the hope he would at last make up his mind to marry her. It would have been wonderful for me. She's like a daughter, and she lives next door. But he was worried because she was so young, and he felt she needed time to grow up, meet other men before she settled down. And then of course he fell in love with you, and suddenly his life is settled. He's made his choice and I'm delighted. I might even live to see some grandchildren after all.'

Davina felt her throat constrict. She should have expected something like this. There was bound to be someone important in Jake's life. Things never worked out to be simple, and she wished herself out of this tangle of lies and heady emotions. She leaned back wearily, all her pleasure in the day gone, as Mr Humphries talked.

'That's really my only wish now, to see a grandson ... or daughter, of course,' he chuckled. 'I'm very dependent on Jake, you see, because he's my only child. He was so wild, you know. For years I was worried sick about him. That was before my illness, after his mother died. You know, he was only eleven. And he adored her. He just couldn't accept that she was dead, gone. He used to roam the countryside all hours of the day and night, couldn't sleep. That was when his insomnia started. He truanted from school, ran away from boarding school when I tried that. Then he wouldn't study, take exams. He didn't want to go to university ... oh, it was terrible. And he had no friends, didn't want any, he said, didn't need anyone. And he always had this bleak haunted look about him. Sometimes it comes back—as you saw this morning when you arrived. I don't know what brings it on or what he's thinking when it happens.' He sighed and his voice faded for a moment.

'And then he found this advertising thing, and that worked for him. Since then he hasn't looked back. He loves his work, as you know. And his boat, of course. That has first place after his work. Everything else has to take second place to that, even women, I sometimes think. But there, that's all over now he has you.'

He sat up suddenly and focused on her, leaning forward to pat her knee. 'Good gracious, I'm sorry! I'm supposed to be pumping you, and here I am talking about myself. Now how about another drink?'

'Excuse me, sir.' An elderly woman stood in the door-way, tall, slim and slightly angular, comfortably dressed in skirt and blouse with flat peep-toe sandals.

'Hello, Bella,' Mr Humphries turned to her, 'come in and meet the fiancée.' He turned back to Davina. 'She only calls me sir when there are visitors,' he said drily. 'This is Davina Richards, Bella, and she's going to marry Jake.'

Mrs Bateman came into the room and stood looking down at Davina.

'I'm pleased to meet you,' she said formally, and Davina felt she was taking stock, making a mental note of everything and filing it away somewhere in her memory.

She smiled 'How do you do, Mrs Bateman.' She spoke evenly, making no pretence of knowledge or feelings she didn't have, and thought she saw a brief look of approval flit across the older woman's face for a moment.

'Mm,' she said, and turned to go. 'I came to ask if young Anita is staying to lunch. I forgot to ask her.'

'I think she has to get back, Bella, and I would guess not.'

'Right,' and she went out again.

Davina got up, feeling rather restless. She wished she could go and explore the garden, and she walked over to the patio doors to look out.

Voices could be heard from the hall and Jake and Anita were back, arms round each other, high colour in their cheeks, laughing.

'Hello, you two.' Jake strode over to the drinks. 'You

look solemn. Have you been exchanging secrets? Anita, your usual?'

He looked magnificent in jodhpurs and polished brown riding boots, an open-necked shirt showing the strong line of his tanned throat and the beginnings of dark hair curling towards his neck.

'Yes, darling, thank you.' Anita took her drink and settled at his feet as he sat down.

'Wow,' Jake breathed, 'I'm certainly out of condition!' His voice was rueful. 'I must get back to my work-outs in London. I've been skipping it lately.' He raised his glass at Davina. 'Other things on my mind,' he said with a wicked glint in his eyes.

She raised her chin at him and he laughed.

'Well, how have you two been getting on?' he asked.

'Too well to be any of your business, young man,' his father replied promptly, 'but don't you think it's time for lunch? Mrs B. can't keep it for ever.'

'Oh, heavens,' Anita exclaimed, 'I must fly. Daddy will skin me alive!' She got up and stretched, showing off her figure to advantage in the cream silk blouse and light brown riding outfit. She looked longingly up at Jake. 'Are we going sailing after lunch, lover? Please?' she begged him. 'Please!'

'Sorry, love, not today. I've an appointment in London tonight, and Davina and I will be leaving soon after lunch. Another time.' His tone brooked no opposition. He got up. 'And now I really must dash upstairs and change, otherwise I'll be in everybody's black books. You two must be starving.'

As he went out Mr Humphries said to Anita, 'Why don't you come over for some coffee after lunch, Nita, if you can?'

'Oh, can I?' She was ecstatic again and rushed over to the wheelchair, flinging her arms round the older man and kissing him firmly on the cheek. 'Super,' she said. 'See you later,' and she ran out into the garden.

Lunch was served by Mrs Bateman in the dining room and was a quiet affair. Father and son chatted casually about the garden, neighbours, a horse that was not well, and Davina was happy to have no demands made on her, content to sit and watch them. The meal was delicious and she enjoyed it—cold salmon served with a fresh herb mayonnaise and home-baked bread with salad. She and Jake drank chilled white wine and Mr Humphries had mineral water. Of the fruit Davina chose melon to follow and ended up with black coffee.

Both men lit cigars and Davina leaned back, at ease and content for the first time for days, only half listening to the men, letting her mind drift. Mrs Bateman came to clear away and Davina rose to help her stack the crockery in the roomy dishwasher in the kitchen.

Jake popped his head round the door and, seeing a pile of newly baked biscuits on the table, came in and sat down, watching them work and helping himself.

'That was a lovely meal, as usual, Bella,' he said casually.

'You're a great one for flattery, Jake, always were,' she said drily, but Davina noted her flushed look of pleasure at his words.

'Darling,' Jake was getting up, 'I'll have to do about half an hour's work and go through that crisps contract before we get back. Sorry to leave you again. Can you amuse yourself for that time, because Dad will be going for his rest.'

'Now don't you worry about Davina,' Mrs Bateman said. 'I'll get her fixed up on the terrace in a lounger and I daresay she'll enjoy a doze. Weddings are always exhausting. Go on, off you go.'

'I don't know how it is,' Jake said in mock alarm, 'but whenever I come home, everyone is forever saying "off you go" to me every few minutes. I wonder why?'

'There's an answer to that,' said Bella.

'O.K.' Jake laughed. 'See you later, darling!' And he went.

The sun was hot and Davina put on her dark glasses. She had taken off her jacket and was enjoying the lazy quiet.

Her eyes were closed and she was almost asleep when Anita's voice woke her.

'Where's Jake?' she demanded.

'Oh . . . er . . . I'm not sure.' Davina sat up. 'I think he said he had some papers to check.'

'How stuffy! That means he'll have locked himself into his study. He always does that when he wants to work undisturbed.'

Davina leaned back, hoping the girl would go and leave her alone.

'I'll go and see if I can dig him out,' Anita said petulantly, and soon after Davina could hear her in the hall.

'Jake . . . Jake, can I come in?' There was a pause. 'I know you're in there, Jake. . . . Please, Jake! I'll be ever so good and quiet. I won't talk or make a sound, I promise. Jake . . . oh,' her voice shrilled petulantly, 'I hate you! Go to hell!' And she came flouncing back to Davina. 'I'm sure he's in there. He just won't answer.'

'Why don't you wait till he comes out?' Davina asked reasonably.

'Why don't you shut up and keep out of it?' Anita said rudely. 'And stop looking so smug,' she went on childishly, 'just because you've got his ring on your finger. You think he's going to marry you, don't you? Well, he won't. He's going to marry me. That was decided years ago, and nothing has changed.'

She stopped, but not for long.

'Oh, yes, he fancies you, I can see that. But that doesn't last. It never does with Jake. And that's not what he wants from a wife.' She continued confidently, 'You see, however many women he picks up in London, he always comes back to me, because he knows no other man has ever touched me, and in the end he doesn't like women like you who've been messed about by other men.'

There was a shocked silence as she finished, and even Anita realised she had gone too far. Davina stood up slowly and faced the girl. She took off her glasses and the cold fury in her eyes was quite frightening.

'I don't know what's eating you up and I don't care.

Your nasty little mind shows that under that little girl act you're probably rather cold. You're certainly insensitive, selfish, noisy and rude. If you think those qualities give you any right to preach to me about love, you're mistaken. Love is about sharing and about caring for the loved person. It's about laughter and silences and warmth and passion. It's not greedy, heedless or selfish.' She breathed in deeply, suddenly strangely confident, and continued with icy calm, 'What I want from the man I love and what I would have to give him is far removed from your childish greed, so don't try to patronise me.'

She looked away from the girl's face, suddenly drawn, straight into Jake's eyes. He was standing quite still in the doorway looking at her, his eyes inscrutable. Her heart leapt into her throat, surprise and shock keeping her still as they gazed at each other in the stillness of the room. And suddenly all uncertainty and confusion dropped away from her. Like a shutter that had obscured her vision and now clicked back into place, she recognised the truth. She loved him.

This strange joy that caught her by the throat at his nearness, this was love. The trembling and the yearning was no infatuation as she had thought. And all the questions were now answered, all the turmoil and depression of the last days explained. She couldn't tear her eyes away from his, heedless of what he might see in her face.

And then Anita moved. With a sob she ran past Jake out into the hall, and Davina shuddered. For a moment she had forgotten everything, the sham engagement, the reason why she was in this house, Jake's love for the young girl who had run away. She turned from him and walked blindly out on to the terrace, into the garden, away from those penetrating eyes that had the power to look into her heart.

She crouched on a stone seat looking out to sea. The sun had disappeared and the wind was blowing up the cliffs, chilling her bare arms. She marvelled that she could have been so blind. Even Philip had guessed. Her sister had seen it and her mother had known.

And she felt only despair. Anita had been right—Jake did not love her. He possibly fancied her, but nothing else. It was Anita he loved and whom he would one day marry, however many women he might desire in passing.

So could she now face an affair with him? Was her love enough to make a success of that? Would it be better than nothing? And what about her job? Could she go on working with him, knowing how she felt, and be on her guard with him day in and day out?

She didn't know the answer to that; she couldn't think.

And she had to get away from Jake, to sort herself out, to find out what was best for her to do. She couldn't face the long drive back to London with him; she would give herself away. He would guess how she felt if he didn't know it already. She would have to find some other way to travel home.

She sensed he was watching her before she turned to see him standing behind her, the wind ruffling his hair.

'We have to go,' he said tonelessly, 'it's getting late.'

'Of course.' Davina rose, feeling stiff and cramped. 'I'll just say my goodbyes.'

'My father is asleep and Mrs Bateman has gone to rest. I've said your goodbyes.'

She walked past him through the house and out to the car. There was no sign of Anita, and she wondered if Jake had spent the last half hour with her, consoling her for what had happened.

He unlocked the car and they got in. 'Oh,' she exclaimed, 'my jacket!'

'It's in the back,' he said indifferently, and switched on the ignition. As they came out of the drive, she turned to him.

'Jake, would you mind taking me to Mevagissey station? I'd like to go back by train.'

He took no notice and drove on. 'Jake,' she tried again, 'did you hear me?'

'Yes, I heard you.' He was angry. 'I just want to get out of sight of the house before we have our next argument.'

She flinched at his words.

'If there's a train at this time on a Sunday and you don't have to wait for hours for it, you realise you won't get home till the early hours. I shall be back long before you.'

'I'm sorry. I don't want to be a nuisance or to make you angry again, but I think perhaps I've had enough of cars. I might not react very well to another long trip.'

'Don't trouble to tell me lies, Davina,' he said coldly. 'I can tell a mile off when you veer away from the truth. I'm not interested in your reasons for not wanting to travel back with me—I can guess. As you no doubt were going to add, our usefulness to each other is over for the moment.' He sighed and ran his hand through his hair. 'I just think it's silly, that's all. We don't have to talk. You can do some more sleeping. I should be able to do it in six hours.'

He looked ahead and turned off the engine. He was slightly slumped in his seat, his face turned away from her, his attitude one of intense weariness.

'Very well,' he said at last, 'if that's what you want, let's try it,' and he drove off. He stopped in the station yard. 'You wait here. I'll see if there's a train.'

Left alone, Davina was regretting her request. She could have had a few more hours with Jake. Instead she had angered him and would have to go home alone. She was stupidly disappointed he had not insisted on her driving home with him. He didn't seem to mind at all. Oh, dear, she thought. If this was love, she wished it had not happened to her.

Jake pulled open the door on her side. 'There's a train in a couple of minutes,' he said. 'If you hurry you can get it. We'll have to run across the track—come on!'

He took her case in one hand and her arm in the other, running with her up the other end of the platform where a gate stood open across the track. It began to close as they went through it.

Arrived on the other platform, they stopped out of breath.

'Here,' said Jake, 'your ticket.'

'Oh, thank you,' she said breathlessly, and looked up at him.

'Davina,' he began, 'will you. . . .' But the whistle of the train stopped him. 'There's the train,' he said harshly above the noise, and they waited till it stopped. He opened a first class compartment and Davina was glad to see it was empty. She turned to take her case.

'Get in,' he commanded, and climbed in after her, putting her case on the rack. As he turned they bumped into each other and for a moment their bodies touched. Jake put out a hand to steady her, and she felt his grip tighten convulsively on her arms. He pressed her tightly to him and she lifted her face.

The warning shout from the guard sounded loud and near, and Jake let her go and jumped swiftly out on to the platform as the guard slammed the door between them.

'Get home safely,' he said gruffly through the open window. Then he turned away, walked rapidly towards the exit and out of sight.

A moment later the train started.

CHAPTER EIGHT

DAVINA got into the office early the next morning and it seemed like any other Monday. She washed up Friday's cups, forgotten by Heather, and put fresh coffee into the machine. Then she sorted the post which had been left unopened on Friday, automatically putting on one side those to be dealt with by Jake personally. These she stacked with the relevant files and took into his office to leave on his desk.

It had been a long night. The train journey had seemed endless, with long stops at almost every station. She had watched the darkening countryside, her mind blank, too tired to think and too dispirited to feel. She had grown cold with only her suit jacket to huddle into; her short fur coat was in the boot of the Rolls. At first she had tried to figure out what she was going to do, but in the end she had dozed fitfully, jolting awake every time the train stopped and the lights flickered, until she had reached Paddington in the early hours. She had been lucky to find a taxi to take her out to Hampstead, and had let herself into the sleeping house, relieved to be home at last.

Dumping her suitcase, she had flung off her clothes, got into a dressing gown and turned on the heating. For a time she had sat with a hot drink and an untouched sandwich, but an hour later, still stupefied, she had crawled into bed, falling asleep within minutes. Restlessly she had tossed and turned, to wake up finally at four o'clock. She had got up, turned on the lights and made herself some coffee.

And then it had hit her. The numbed feeling had gone with sleep and warmth. The fog had cleared from her mind, and the pain began.

She loved Jake. And she would have to leave him, find another job. Philip had said all secretaries fell in love with their bosses, but they didn't all marry them. And he had been right.

Philip. She suddenly realised it was twenty-four hours since she had given him a thought. Her feelings for him she now dismissed as the dream Jake had said they were; Jake had been right about so much. Perhaps she had loved Philip once, but not the way she now loved Jake. Philip had not been real as Jake was now.

She loved and wanted Jake physically, but there was so much more. She wanted to be with him, to laugh with him and talk, to have him take care of her, and she wanted him to need her as she needed him. She thought ironically how easy it was to decide what one wanted. It was far more difficult to face the thought of having to do without it.

There was no way she could have an affair with him, even if that was what he wanted. And she was by no means sure if he did want it. Perhaps the week-end and a few kisses were quite enough for him. After all, he now had Andrea Temple to go back to. Anyway, it didn't make much difference either way.

She would have to get right away from him, from London perhaps. In time the pain would go or lessen, and she would be able to make some kind of life without him.

'Good morning, Davina.' It was Jake. 'You're early this morning.'

He didn't stop, but breezed straight through into his own office, not giving her a glance. She sat down on rather wobbly legs, and decided to stop dreaming and start work. There was plenty to do. She switched off the coffee and sat at her desk, trying not to think about the silence from the other room. Then she began to work. After a few minutes she was completely engrossed. When Heather arrived at nine o'clock, Davina greeted her quite naturally.

'Good week-end?' Heather asked.

'Yes, thank you. Everything all right on Friday?' Davina queried.

'Sure thing.' Heather was feeling chatty. 'Did you know the boss was away on Friday as well?'

The intercom flicked. 'Davina?'

'Yes?'

'Can I have some coffee, please?'

'Yes, right away.' Davina switched off the intercom. 'Heather, would you please go down for the post? I'll take in the coffee.'

'Right,' and Heather bounced out.

Davina poured Jake's coffee and went straight into his office without knocking. She put the cup down on his desk and he looked up briefly.

'Thank you.' Then she saw him stiffen. 'Where's your ring?' he demanded. 'Your engagement ring, Davina. Have you lost it?'

'No, of course not,' she said hotly. 'I've taken it off.'

'Why?' he demanded flatly.

'Don't you remember?' she stammered. 'We agreed. . . .'

'Agreed what?'

'That I wouldn't wear it in the office.'

'Did we? I don't remember that.' He sat back and looked at her, noting the white face, the deep shadows under the eyes. 'I have your fur jacket,' he said suddenly. 'It's in the car.'

'Oh, yes,' she said. 'Er . . . could I talk to you for a moment, please?'

'Certainly,' he said curtly. 'We're having dinner tonight. I'll pick you up at seven-thirty.'

'No!' Her voice was sharply anxious. 'Please . . . I mean now. Could I talk to you for a minute?'

'No.' His voice was cold. 'I have this meeting in an hour and piles of stuff to get through before then. After that I'll be out for the rest of the day. I can't stop now.'

He was waiting for her to leave. But she didn't want to have dinner with him.

'I'm afraid I can't manage tonight,' she said next.

'Well then, I won't be able to find time to talk to you . . . or to listen, for that matter,' Jake said coldly.

Davina bit her lip uncertainly.

'Oh, for goodness' sake, Davina,' he snapped, 'we've had several meals together. You should know I don't eat girls over the dinner table.'

The colour flooded her face, but he didn't notice. He was looking down at his papers, pen in hand, a heavy frown between his eyes.

'Well, can you break your date? I can't wait around while you go off into a dream.'

'Very well,' she said heavily.

'Good, that's settled, then. Can I get on now, please?'

'More wine, *signore, signorina*?' The waiter was hovering.

'No, I think not,' said Jake. 'Coffee and liqueur . . . Davina, apricot brandy?'

She nodded. He remembered from the dinner dance that it was the only liqueur she liked.

'One apricot brandy and a Rémy Martin for me, please,' Jake ordered.

'Immediately, Signor Humphries.'

'Thank you, Jake,' said Davina. 'I enjoyed that. It was a really lovely meal.'

'Good.' He looked at her. 'That's the first smile I've had out of you all evening.'

She was fiddling with her wine glass, a little nervous. He took it from her and picked up her left hand, playing idly with the finger where her ring had been. His touch was playing havoc with her senses, and she remembered the feeling of his parted lips against her palm in the kitchen at home.

'Now would you like to tell me what you were bursting with this morning?' he asked.

He had refused to let her talk when they arrived. Davina looked round the exclusive Italian restaurant where they were dining in an alcove, almost completely cut off from the other diners. It was the first time Jake had taken her out on a date, and she reflected ruefully that it was also the last. She had determined to enjoy it to the full. They had talked easily, joking about people and events over the week-end, gossiping about shop talk for a while, and all without tensions. Jake had been amusing, entertaining, and had not caused her a moment's embarrassment.

She had had to promise him at the start of the evening that nothing serious would be discussed over dinner—and now they had finished eating and the moment had come.

'Goodness, is it that difficult?' he asked, smiling faintly.

'It is a little, partly because I don't like what I'm going to say.'

'Well then, don't say it,' he said coldly.

'I have to.' She took a deep breath. 'I would like you to accept my notice. As soon as you can find a replacement for me, I want to leave the agency.'

'Oh, is that all?' Jake sighed with relief. 'I agree with you, it's the best thing under the circumstances. In fact I was going to suggest it myself.'

She looked at him astounded. He wanted her to go. He wasn't going to try and stop her going. She couldn't believe it.

'You see,' he went on smoothly, 'I wanted you to come out with me this evening for a reason, and what you've told me fits in rather well with my own plans.'

She looked at him now with curiosity, wondering what was coming next. He stopped playing with her finger and took her hand in a firm clasp. She tried to pull away, but he tightened his hold.

'Davina, will you consider making our engagement a real one? I would like us to be married when you've had time to get used to the idea.'

She stared at him, blindly, unable to take in what he had said.

'I don't understand,' she whispered at last.

'It doesn't seem complicated to me,' he said coolly. 'This is a proposal of marriage.' He smiled at her rather mockingly. 'The usual answer is either yes or no.'

'You can't mean it,' she said thickly. 'It has to be some kind of joke.'

'Do you know that's almost exactly what you said the

last time I proposed?'

'But . . . why . . .?' she stammered awkwardly.

'All the usual reasons why people get married,' Jake said lightly. 'I believe we have much in common. We get on. You understand about my work, the long hours, the travelling. You would be able to entertain my business contacts. I think I'm not being unreasonably conceited if I say that we seem to find each other attractive. I would like to start a family in the not too distant future, if the idea appeals to you. That seems already to be a lot more reasons than most people have these days for getting married.'

'I'm sorry, I. . . .' Davina began.

'Just before you say no again, Davina, think a minute. I'm not asking you to marry me tomorrow. I hope I can persuade you in time to see it as a good idea. In the meantime I'd like you to wear my ring. But there won't be any rush to get married. There'll be plenty of time to get used to the idea, for us to get to know each other.' He stopped and looked intently into her face. 'Unless of course you have other plans . . . er . . . with someone else.' He stopped, a harsh note in his voice that jarred on her.

Davina felt as though he'd thrown her into a whirlpool. She loved him. There was nothing on this earth she wanted more than to be his wife, to be loved by him. But that was not on offer. His offer sounded like an invitation to dinner. His idea of marriage seemed to be an arrangement rather like hiring a hostess who would be the mother of his children, all thrown in and rolled into one.

She sat rigid with horror at the idea. She would adore him, and he would live his own life just as Monica had prophesied, with the Andrea Temples of this world, and they would meet to discuss his work and the next dinner party. Probably, she thought, slightly hysterical, he would be quite happy for her to have a string of lovers, too. But what about love? Did he plan to live without that for the rest of his life? And what about Anita? How did she fit into this? Was she not good enough to act the hostess, to mother his children? What sort of relationship did he plan to have with her?

'Well, Davina, is there someone else with whom you're involved?' he drawled.

'Jake, I . . .' she tried to explain, 'I'm honoured that you should ask me, but the answer is definitely no. I don't need to think about it. My answer would be no different in weeks or even months from now.' She sounded unhappy, and knew she was close to tears. 'I'm sorry, so sorry,' she added miserably.

'I see,' he said tersely. She looked up to see his face had gone white and taut, and she realised she had made him very angry. She opened her bag and took out the box with his ring inside it, and put it on the table between them. She spoke slowly and with difficulty.

'I think in the circumstances it will be best if we tell our families that we aren't . . . that we decided not to get married after all.'

'No, Davina, I don't want it back. For God's sake, you keep it.' His voice was raw and she kept her eyes down, refusing to look at him.

'I couldn't keep it. I'm sorry, Jake, it's not possible.'

'Oh, dear God, woman, why can't you . . .' He took the box and she saw his hand clench over it till the knuckles showed white. Her eyes flew to his face, but he was looking down at his hand, and she couldn't see his eyes. He seemed to be fighting for control.

At last he took the box and slipped it into his pocket. 'Very well, that seems to be that, then.' His voice was totally without any of the emotion of moments earlier, and Davina thought she must have imagined his agitation.

'I wish it could be different,' she said quietly, almost to herself.

'Do you? Do you really?' He leaned over and grasped her wrist. 'Well, why can't it be different? Are you marching straight into an affair with your brother-in-law? Is that why you can't get married?'

'No!' Her voice was anguished. 'No, Jake, how could you? Oh, God, no, of course not!' She couldn't take any more of this. 'Please, I would like to go.'

'Yes, of course.'

Jake signalled for the bill, and within minutes they were outside in Mayfair. In silence he put her into the car and drove her home. Outside her house he stopped the engine and switched off the lights.

'Thank you for tonight, Jake,' she said quietly. 'I'm sorry it had to end this way.'

'It hasn't ended yet,' he said angrily, and gripped her shoulders, pulling her into his arms.

'No,' she thought, 'I can't cope with this, not tonight,' and she fought him, trying to pull away, punching at him with her fists. But she made no impression on him. He held her so securely that she couldn't wrench away. Then he bent his head and stopped her cry with his mouth, pressing her lips in a possessive kiss that had her gasping for air. But he didn't let up, forcing her lips apart, kissing her hungrily as though he would never let her go, and she couldn't go on withholding her response. Suddenly she was kissing him back, fiercely and longingly, and she heard him groan her name. He kissed her hair, her eyes, her throat. She heard the buttons rip as he pulled her dress open and bent to kiss her shoulder, his tongue leaving a trail of fire as his mouth returned to her lips, opening them with his own. She was clinging to him, wanting him, yearning for him to take her.

He put his hand down to the soft skin of her breast, and she felt the nipple harden at his touch. And suddenly with a rush her mind returned to sanity and with a sob she pulled herself away from him.

He wasn't expecting it, and in a moment she was free. She grabbed for the door handle, pulled open the door and was running to the house, hunting feverishly for her key in case Jake was following. She let herself in, sped up the stairs to her own flat and locked herself in, leaning breathlessly against the door.

There was not a sound. She didn't hear the car start, and she was sure he hadn't gone. Was something wrong? She had not looked back in her headlong flight. Was he all right? Had she unwittingly hurt him as she tore herself away?

She opened her door and went along the landing to the window that gave on to the street. The car was still there and the lights were out. Oh, God, she thought, he was hurt! Unthinkingly, she rushed downstairs and out.

As she opened the front door she saw him. He was standing by the side of the car, smoking a cigar, looking up at the house.

'Jake,' she said softly, 'are you all right?'

'Davina,' he said quietly, 'will you come here a moment?'

She moved and stood before him, looking up into his face.

'I think it's better if we don't meet again,' he said in a low voice. 'There's no need to work your notice. I'll manage with temporary help until I find someone. I'll explain that you're not well and have taken leave of absence. After a time, I'll inform Personnel that you won't be coming back. That way there should be no problems for you.' He threw away his cheroot and opened the car door. 'Thank you for coming down again,' he said, got in and drove away.

Davina had been prepared for the beginning to be bad, but nothing had prepared her for the pain, the terrible sense of loss, the emptiness.

After the first twenty-four hours she decided she needed a holiday. She wouldn't try to look for work. But it was all useless. She couldn't sleep or rest, and her mind was totally concentrated on Jake.

Had she made the right decision? Would it have been better to be married to him, whatever kind of marriage he wanted, than to be totally without him? Could she have got used to his terms? Perhaps in time they would have come to a closer relationship. He might even have learned to love her.

Those would be her thoughts in the darkness of night.

By the morning she had changed her mind. She had done the right thing. The raw pain of being with Jake, unloved, watching him with other women, was unthinkable agony, worse than being without him. And all the time she missed him. During the day she wanted to tell him things she noticed, hear him laugh, watch him smile, eat with him, and nothing seemed to make sense without him.

But the nights were the worst. That first week was made up of the longest nights she had ever lived through. She tossed and turned, longing for him physically. She wanted him there in her bed, holding her, loving her. She would never have thought it possible that she could yearn for someone so deeply.

Looking back, it seemed incredible that she had worked with him all that time without feeling anything for him, that three days out of her life could have riveted her deepest feelings and committed her to him so completely.

She had told Mrs Blunt nothing and, blessedly her landlady had asked no questions. She took messages on the telephone, swearing blind that Miss Richards was away and she couldn't say where she had gone. Once a day she would come up to the flat with the post and bring messages. Sometimes she would arrive with a cup of tea which she had just happened to be making, a plate of soup or a piece of pie. She never stopped, never came in and never asked questions.

Heather rang several times, so did Mike and Georgina. But Davina never rang back; she wanted no contact with any of them, and hoped they would eventually get tired of trying to contact her, and stop.

After a week she started going out. One evening she went to the cinema and found herself crying in the middle of a rather sophisticated comedy, so she came away.

Then she started getting up in the night to go for drives. She went up to Whitestone Pond, down to the Embankment or into the deserted West End. And that helped. She began to see London and grew to love it. The town seemed to come into its own in the early hours. The street lamps shone on the newly washed roads as the sweepers went slowly by. Shops were shrouded in darkness and traffic lights flickered on and off into a world empty of cars and people. After such drives she would come home exhausted and able to sleep. With no alarm clock set and no reason to get up, she would sleep on into the day.

She found she was losing weight, so she tried going for long walks on the Heath to work up an appetite. She saw fathers on Parliament Hill Fields teaching small sons to fly a kite, endless pram and dog owners watching over their charges, and she spent one whole afternoon playing baseball with half a dozen truanting schoolboys, who accepted her coming and going with complete detachment.

It was the fifth week after her dinner with Jake that she got up to find her little balcony flooded with sunlight. Her spirits lightened and she went out. She bought herself some rolls and coffee in one of the Hampstead tea-shops, and sat outside in the sun, reading a paper.

It turned into a heatwave and Davina loved it. She sat on her balcony, lulled by the sun on her face, thinking of nothing, her mind a blank. And gradually the rawness of the pain began to ease. The longing and the need for him remained, but the desperation lessened. She knew she had to survive without him, and she knew she had to start living again.

The next morning she went to see Maddy. Madeleine Bell, or M.B. as she was known affectionately to her 'girls', ran an employment agency. She handled only girls who wanted temporary work. She had all the best girls in south London, and she allowed them to work for only the very select firms.

All the fifty girls on her books she knew personally, their problems, their private lives and their abilities. She looked after them like a mother hen, and they adored her. She got them jobs by the hour, the day, the week or the month, and all the girls were picked and matched to the jobs. If Nessa didn't like scruffy offices, then Nessa only went to work in Knightsbridge with wall-to-wall carpeting. If Amelia wanted to be paid in cash because she had never got round to having a bank account, then her money was there for her in cash. If they were good and reliable workers, then Maddy would pander to their little weaknesses to keep them happy.

Every Friday afternoon and well into the evening Maddy served chilled white wine, tea and coffee. All the girls came trooping in for their money, for details of the next week's jobs and to tell Maddy their troubles. And she listened, sympathised and understood.

Maddy also made a great deal of money. Her clients trusted her to supply them with good, reliable 'temps', and this she did. All her girls worked hard. They could be trusted, were punctual and had the skills for which they were being paid. Any long lunch hours, or filing nails during working hours, and that was it—a polite goodbye from Maddy and no more jobs.

Somewhere in Maddy's background there was an adoring and much loved husband, but he never appeared when the girls were there on Fridays, and she never talked about him. She herself was darkly good-looking, in her mid-thirties, and was planning to leave 'all this' one day to have babies. But not yet, she always added, not quite yet.

They had met when Davina first came to London from Cornwall and she had worked for Maddy for some weeks before going to join Foster Patterson. When Davina walked in Maddy remembered her immediately. She took one look at Davina's face and got out the white wine, always ready chilled.

'O.K.,' she said without any introductory chit-chat. 'What happened?'

And Davina told her. For the first time she told someone everything. It seemed to pour out of her like a flood, leaving her slightly lightheaded. Maddy just listened and didn't say a word until Davina had finished. And then she made no comment, offered no sympathy or advice. Instead she started cheerfully opening books, looking at lists.

'If you decide to work for me, I shall be only too pleased,' she said brightly. 'There's always plenty of work about at this time of the year with holidays coming up.' She looked at Davina. 'But you've had it good, you know. Do you think you'll be able to slog away typing, making tea, filing endlessly after the interesting and responsible work you've had?'

'That's just what I do want,' Davina pleaded, 'mechanical routine work where I don't have to think or make decisions, and where I'll be able to leave on the dot every night.'

'Very well.' Maddy was sceptical. 'I don't think you'll stick it, but we'll give it a whirl. Now, are you going to insist on being local in Hampstead, because it's not my area.'

'No, I don't mind travelling. I've got a car, if I can afford to go on running it.'

'My dear, if you're prepared to work, every day and all day, you'll make a bomb. And you'll be a star in my heaven. Experienced, attractive personal assistants looking for temporary work don't usually come my way.'

'Maddy,' Davina hesitated, 'will I need ... I mean, can you place me without a reference?'

Maddy looked at her keenly. 'Why? Don't you think your precious Jake will give you one?'

'No, it's not that exactly. I'd rather ... I mean, I'd feel happier if I didn't. . . .'

'You don't want to ask him, and you don't want him to know where you're working,' Maddy said matter-of-factly. 'No, you won't need a reference with me. And after the first week you'll have one if you want it.'

'Oh, Maddy, you're a genius! You make me feel better already.'

'There's nothing like being appreciated and having money in the bank. And both those things you'll start having a week today.' Maddy looked up from her filing cards. 'Take it from an old campaigner, if you don't have to think twice about the price of a ravishing new outfit or a smashing handbag, life is still worth living.'

Davina laughed out loud for the first time in weeks.

And so she began to work for Maddy. The only conditions Davina made were no advertising work and no job for longer than a week. Maddy promised her that and stuck to it. And life began to take on a new rhythm.

Every Monday she was in a different office, with new people, doing vaguely different things. By the time she was on top of the job, familiar with the people and close to boredom, it was Friday and she was leaving.

Strangely, she found it exhilarating to be so entirely without any responsibility. She met a lot of people, and never stayed long enough anywhere to invite curiosity or fend off personal questions.

She got into Maddy's Friday afternoon habit and enjoyed watching the other girls. If she wanted to talk to Maddy, she knew she could do so. But mostly she just went to sit and listen. One or two of the debby girls noted her expensive clothes and tried to become friendly. But this Davina did not encourage.

The weeks went by, and it was summer, nearly three months since she had left Foster Patterson. She was sleeping again almost normally, and she was eating regularly. If she had ever doubted her feelings for Jake that was long past. The raw pain had gone, and she could think of him without trembling. But the strength of her love and her need didn't seem to change. She could feel no interest in any other man. Several tried to date her in the various offices where she worked, but she had never wanted to go out with any of them, not even for an occasional evening out.

Any tall dark-haired man always caught her attention. If the likeness was more striking, her heart would accelerate its beat, and she would half hope, half dread it might be Jake, that she might catch a glimpse of him. But she never did.

And then one hot and balmy lunchtime when Davina was having a sandwich in the park, her slumbering feelings were rudely awakened once more.

'Davina!' said a familiar voice, and she turned to see Heather a few paces away. She was with a young man, and they were holding hands.

'It is, isn't it?' Heather said breathlessly, leaving her companion to rush up to Davina.

'Hello, Heather.' Davina's voice was friendly and cool.

'Gosh,' Heather went on, 'this is a stroke of luck, running into you at last. We've all been wondering about you so often, and nobody seemed to have heard from you. Oh, sorry, this is Andy . . . Davina Richards.' She turned to the young man. 'We used to work together at the agency.'

Davina nodded. 'How do you do.'

The pleasant curly-haired youngster smiled and then turned to Heather. 'I expect you'll want a chat and I'd be in the way. I'll pop down to the lake for a few minutes, and then we must get back.'

'Right, Andy. Thanks.' Heather gave him a hug and a shove in one movement. 'Oh, do let's sit down.' Heather was rushing her words in the same old way. 'How are you? And what have you been doing with yourself? Are you quite better? And are you still working in London? Why haven't any of us seen you?'

Davina laughed. 'Good old Heather! Just the same. Which question shall I answer first?'

'Oh, never mind my questions. Just tell me about yourself.'

Davina hesitated and looked down at her hands.

'If you want to, that is,' Heather added less confidently.

'Yes, well . . .' Davina said slowly, 'I can launch into all sorts of news, but your young man will be back shortly. I'd much rather hear about everyone at the agency. How are Mike and Charlie?' she asked, deliberately avoiding the mention of Jake's name.

'They're both well, although Charlie's going for interviews like mad at the moment, looking for a job. He's leaving.'

Davina was genuinely astonished. 'But why? I can't imagine him leaving the unit.'

'Yes, well, things have . . . they've changed, you know. I mean, it's all very different now.'

Davina was curious, but did not want to show it. Her pulse quickened. Could something have happened to Jake? Had he left?

'What do you mean changed?' she said eventually.

'Well, you know about Miss Durant? You met her, didn't you? I can't remember.'

'No, I never actually met her,' Davina said quietly.

'Yes, well, she's very different from you.'

'Well, she was bound to be,' Davina said drily.

'Oh!' Heather was confused for the moment, and then laughed. 'What I mean is, she's terrifically efficient . . . not that you weren't, of course, but she does it differently. It's all sort of . . . serious.' Heather paused, trying to find the right words.

'I see,' Davina said demurely, 'meaning that I was always shrieking with mirth?'

'Oh, Davina you are a tonic! It's so lovely to see you, like old times. We've all missed you so dreadfully.'

All? Davina wondered. 'Well,' she said lightly, 'I'm flattered, of course, but you haven't told me how everything's changed.'

'Well, it's not just Miss Durant who never laughs or has a joke. It's Jake, too.'

He is still there then, Davina thought, her pulse fluttering at the mention of his name. 'He's not ill, is he?' she asked carefully.

'Oh, no, nothing like that. It's just that he's so changed. I mean, of course he was always a bit tricky to work for . . . you know, one never knew if he was going to laugh when you made a mistake or if he was going to rip you down.'

'As far as I remember,' Davina said drily, 'that rather depended on the mistake.'

'There you go again! You see? You always see the funny side, and I didn't really appreciate that till you'd gone.'

Heather sounded forlorn.

'You were telling me how Jake had changed,' Davina reminded her.

'Oh, yes. Now he's always on his high horse. I can't remember when any of us had a chat or a laugh with him. He works like a fiend, and he expects us to go on till we drop. And we never have any light relief like we used to in the old days.' Heather sounded perplexed. 'It's not easy to describe what I mean. He's just so bad-tempered all the time.'

'Bad-tempered? I don't remember him ever being that.'

'Yes, well, that's just it. He is now—bad-tempered, I mean. And Charlie says it's almost as though he can't enjoy anything himself and is taking it out on us. Charlie says it's because there seems to be no Andrea Temple around at the moment and that's the trouble. But Mike says there've been times before when there's been no one, and he wasn't like this.'

'Oh, dear,' Davina was thinking out loud, 'maybe he's just going through a bad patch. Or perhaps Miss Durant is taking time to settle. Don't forget I had Georgina when I started.'

'Mm, yes, maybe,' Heather was not convinced, 'but if that was it, you'd think she'd let me help her. But she won't have it. It has to be done by her and in her way. . . . Oh, and she hates to have your name mentioned. I learned that in the first week.'

'Yes, well . . . you still haven't told me why Charlie is leaving. That can't be because of Miss Durant.'

'Oh, no, of course not. He and Jake had a fight.'

'A fight?' Davina was incredulous now. 'But Jake never fights with anyone!'

'Well, exactly, that's what we all said afterwards, and Mike told Charlie to ignore the whole thing, that Jake was upset and wasn't himself. But Charlie was livid.'

'Oh, dear,' Davina said again, noting all the "Charlie saids" and "Mike saids" that seemed to litter Heather's conversation.

'It was all rather odd, really.' Heather wrinkled her brow, trying to remember. 'We were having coffee in the office. I'd just made some for the boss, and the boys came in to see him. He had the engaged sign up and I said something about waiting, and Mike said what about a free cup of coffee, then. Anyway, the three of us were drinking coffee when Jake came out of his office and saw us. And . . . oh, yes, I'd forgotten that bit, we were talking about you . . . that's funny, I've only just remembered that. Charlie was saying he'd seen Georgina and the baby and that they were hoping you'd be visiting . . . something like that. And Jake turned on Charlie, absolutely furious. I've never seen him so angry. He was quite white with it, I remember. He said he couldn't see the point of their being employed by him if all they could do was to waste his time, drinking his coffee and making so much noise with idle chat in his office that he couldn't work. Well, you could have heard a pin drop. . . .' Heather turned to Davina, who had gone strangely rigid in the face. 'Are you all right, Davina? You look a bit funny.'

'Yes, yes, I'm fine. What happened then?'

'Well, for a minute nobody moved or said anything. It was awful, and Jake just stood there, blazing with anger. I've never seen him like that before.'

Davina said nothing. She felt her throat constrict. Heather went on.

'And then Charlie lost his temper, and he told Jake what he could do with his lousy job, and that he, Charlie could spend his coffee break as he pleased, and if he didn't like the way he was doing his job, then he, Jake, might as well know that he didn't think he was making a particularly good job of his own work any more. . . . Oh, dear, that's a bit muddled, but it was such a shock. I've never seen Charlie lose his temper.'

She stopped, distressed, remembering it all, and then she sighed. 'Anyway, Mike tried to talk Charlie out of leaving. He said Jake was sure to regret what he'd said, and that Charlie should go and see him, but Charlie refused. He said nobody talks to him like that. Anyway, it's affected everyone—first you and now Charlie. I don't blame you for going. I never knew Jake could be like that.'

'Now, Heather, that's nonsense. You know my leaving had nothing whatever to do with Jake,' Davina said deliberately. She looked at her watch. 'I'm afraid I must be going.'

'Oh, but you haven't told me anything about yourself. Here I've been going on about us. Please tell me quickly what you're doing. The others will want to know, too.'

'I'd like to, Heather, but my lunch hour is up, and I must be going. And your Andy is on his way back. He seems nice. Is it serious?'

'Good heavens, Davina, you sound about ninety! Just like my mother. No, it isn't serious. He's nice and we have fun, that's all. Nothing is for ever, you know.'

They stood up to wait for Andy.

'Hello, spitfire,' he said casually. 'We have to go.'

Davina held out her hand. 'It's been nice seeing you, Heather. Give my love to . . . er . . . everyone,' she ended up rather awkwardly. Nodding to Andy, she turned and walked away across the grass towards the park exit.

The afternoon passed in a daze for Davina, and she was glad she had only mechanical jobs to get through. Over and over she thought about the things Heather had told her. Why was Jake impatient and short-tempered? Did it have anything to do with her? Did he miss her at work? But she dismissed that. He knew where she lived; all he had to do was contact her. And he'd made no move to keep her, ask her to stay on. No, whatever was wrong had nothing to do with her.

There was no point in dreaming about what might have been. That way lay more heartache. She had to be strong and put Jake out of her mind again. It was over, definitely over. But she wished she hadn't met Heather. It was all more difficult now. Her longing for him suddenly intensified, and she was swept headlong into a tidal wave of misery, like a throbbing pain now vibrantly alive again.

She felt alone and desolate, as though she had to begin the forgetting battle all over again.

The telephone was ringing as she opened the front door, and she reached for it automatically.

'Hello.'

'Davina?'

'Yes, who is that?'

'It's Georgina. I'm so glad I've got you at last. Where have you been hiding yourself? I've tried so often to catch you on the phone.'

'I'm sorry, Georgina . . . how are you? And the baby? And Larry?'

'Oh, we're all well, thanks. Listen, I don't want to keep you chatting now, but you are coming on Saturday, aren't you? I wanted to make sure.'

'Saturday?' queried Davina.

'The christening, love, don't you remember? Only you haven't answered the invitation.' There was a moment's silence. 'You are coming, Davina, aren't you? Please don't say no. We do want to see you. Quite apart from the baby and the christening . . . say you'll come.'

'Well, it's rather difficult because I'm supposed to be going home for the week-end,' Davina improvised on the spur of the moment.

'Well, that should be possible,' Georgina calculated.' The christening is at eleven-thirty, and we're having people back here for a buffet lunch. You can still get away quite early after that.'

Davina felt mean, not wanting to go. 'All right,' she said rather weakly, 'I'll make it. And thank you for asking me.'

'Good.' Georgina became brisk and businesslike. 'Listen, there are going to be masses of people, but I do want to talk to you alone. I'll corner you at lunch and ask you to come up and see Adam with me. Then we can have a quick chat away from the crowd.'

'Yes, of course. See you Saturday, then.'

''Bye . . . and oh, Davina, you won't change your mind and pull out at the last moment, will you?'

Davina laughed lightly. 'No, I won't, even if I'm tempted,' she said, and rang off.

After she'd hung up she was frightened. It was a mistake to go. There was bound to be talk about Jake and everyone from the office would be there. He might even be there himself. Then she chided herself for foolishness. After all, babies and churches were definitely not in his line. It was extremely unlikely that he would be there.

CHAPTER NINE

WHEN she arrived at the church Jake was the first person she saw, and a sudden irrational joy pierced her at the sight of him. Not only did he tower over most of the men there, but he was standing at Larry's side at the font, one of Adam godfathers.

The small church was full and beautifully decorated with flowers and fern, reminding Davina of the last time she had been in church, at her sister's wedding. That time Jake had been at her side.

She was late, and the family were grouped round the vicar, Georgina holding Adam in her arms. Jake had his back to her, and she could see the achingly familiar set of his shoulders and the back of his head with the crisp hair neatly dressed. As the ceremony progressed and the godparents took their vows, Davina became more and more conscious of him. She could think of nothing else, and was grateful she had time to compose herself for the inevitable meeting. She wondered briefly if she could escape at the end of the service and skip the lunch. She was still dithering about that when the ceremony ended and she walked slowly out with the rest of the congregation.

At least she had dressed carefully and knew she looked her best in a pale soft green georgette dress with full pleaded skirt and matching coat. A small chiffon-covered picture hat in a toning shade enhanced the grey of her eyes and shadowed the rich auburn of her silky hair coiled into a soft and heavy knot.

At the reception everything was a blur. She was immediately surrounded by old mates. Mike and Susan were there with the girls, Charlie and a girl-friend chatted and joked, and Davina forced herself to concentrate on them, what they were saying and how they looked. She refused to allow her eyes to roam the room to find Jake.

Then for a moment she was alone, gazing unseeingly down at plates of tempting snacks, holding a champagne glass in her hand. Speeches and toasts were over, and people were wandering about, laughing and chatting.

'Hello, Davina.'

She looked up straight into Jake's face. 'Hello, Jake,' she said quietly.

'How are you?' he asked next.

'Fine, thank you.' Davina found her throat constricted. After that first glance she stared as if hypnotised down into her glass.

'Have you come up for the day for this do, or are you staying over?' he asked.

She looked up at that. 'What do you mean?' she asked stupidly. Where was she supposed to have come up from? Hampstead? She looked at him. He was as always impeccably dressed in a pale grey lightweight silk suit with a darker grey shirt and light tie. He seemed to have lost weight and his height was even more pronounced because he was thinner. His face was still tanned, but he looked tired, with deep shadows under his eyes and lines between his brows and from the strong nose down to his mouth, drawn into a grim line that accentuated the jutting chin. The thick dark hair had new white streaks in it, and his eyes were veiled, guarded. Davina wasn't sure if he was bored, but he didn't look well.

'Can I fill up your glass?' His voice was polite.

'No, thank you,' she said. 'I have to be going.'

'Can I give you a lift anywhere?' he asked sharply.

'Thank you,' she said in the same polite voice, 'I have my own car here.'

'Yes, of course.' He paused for an awkward moment. 'No doubt you're heading straight out of London in this lovely weather.'

'As a matter of fact I am, yes.' She looked up at him. 'Are you?'

'No, I'm staying in London,' he said curtly.

'Er ... how is your father?' Davina asked next, wishing this awful conversation would end and not knowing quite how to finish it.

'Not very well.'

'Oh, I'm sorry,' she said, forgetting the awkwardness between them. 'Is it serious?'

'We're not sure yet,' he replied, his look suddenly intent, so that she had to look down to hide the blush that was creeping into her face. 'He's in a London hospital undergoing tests to see if he really needs this operation.'

'Oh, please,' Davina said urgently, 'will you tell him. . . .'

'He would like very much to see you,' Jake interrupted harshly, 'but I told him you wouldn't have the time and you'd probably be in Cornwall.'

She bit her lip nervously. 'Oh, but I . . . I'd like to see him, to visit, if he really wants me to. Which hospital is it?'

'He would like that,' said Jake, his voice no longer cold. 'In fact I shall be going on there from this do. If you'd care to come with me I could take you and deliver you back here to your car. It's St Thomas's . . . not very far.'

He was waiting, suddenly tense, for her answer. She turned her face to his and their eyes locked. For a moment tension seemed to throb between them and the guards were down. Davina felt as if she was drowning in emotion, and she didn't know if it was his or hers. More than she'd ever wanted anything in her life, she wanted his arms round her and his body close to hers, to run her hands through his hair and to feel his mouth against her lips. The strength of her own feelings frightened her with their intensity.

'Well, you two,' said a gay, familiar voice, 'aren't you eating?'

Davina dragged her eyes away from Jake, as Georgina put an arm round each of them affectionately. She blushed a fiery red and tried to hide her embarrassment.

'I'm afraid I'm not really very hungry,' she said brightly.

'It has to be that. You can't be dieting—I've never

seen you so thin.' Georgina turned to Jake.

'I shall have to tear her away from you for a little while,' she said. 'Davina has promised to help me with something upstairs.'

Jake had withdrawn his gaze and was looking round the room. Davina wondered if Anita was with him. She hadn't seen her in church, but she might well be here.

He nodded coolly to both of them. 'I'll take myself off, then,' he drawled. 'I wouldn't want to interfere with girlish confidences. If you'll both excuse me, I'll find Larry and say my goodbyes.'

Georgina put her hand on his arm. 'Thank you, Jake, for everything,' she said affectionately. She stood on tiptoe and kissed him lightly on the cheek. 'Bless you . . . and take care of yourself.'

She took her hand away and he was gone.

As Davina followed her from the room and up the stairs to the nursery, she felt in a turmoil. She was walking and talking quite mechanically, her mind and her heart still with Jake, wherever he was at that moment.

Georgina opened the door to a sunny bedroom, windows open to the afternoon breeze with cot and toys and chests neatly tidy against a pretty pale blue wallpaper and rugs underfoot on the polished parquet floor.

'We won't be disturbed here because Mum has Adam in her bedroom for a bit. He was so good in church that he's quite exhausted and has dropped off to sleep on her bed. She'll sit patiently watching to make sure he doesn't roll off.' She looked rather searchingly at Davina's pale face. 'Let's sit down for·a minute. It's not too comfortable, but I do want to see you without interruptions, and almost everywhere in the house today someone is sure to pop in unexpectedly.'

'Adam's so gorgeous, you must be terribly proud of him . . . and Larry,' Davina said, smiling.

'Yes, I'm lucky. Larry wanted a boy, because he feels he's starting a family rather late. I just wanted a healthy baby, and that I have. But that's not what I want to talk about.'

She hesitated. 'Davina, I want to talk to you about Jake.'

'No!' Davina couldn't help the agonised explanation 'I mean . . . really, I don't want to go into the whole business of why I left Fosters. . . .' She smiled rather mistily at the other girl.

'I don't mean Foster Patterson,' said Georgina. I would have to be blind not to see what you two feel for each other. I interrupted because I thought you might actually start making love right there and then in a room full of people.'

'Oh, dear!' Davina blushed. 'I'm sorry, am I that obvious?'

'My dear, it's not only you. It's him, too.'

'No, unfortunately not,' Davina said quietly.

'That's what I want to discuss. How much do you know about Jake?' asked Georgina. Davina looked at her questioningly. 'I mean how much do you know about his family life, his past?'

'I don't know much about his past. I've met his family . . . his father.'

'I wonder if you know about Linda?' Georgina asked.

'Linda?' Davina echoed.

'Linda was a staggeringly beautiful teenager. I only met her years after Jake knew her, but even then she was ravishing. And she had it all . . . looks, brains, money. When Jake met her he must have been about twenty-three or four, and she was seventeen. He adored her. She was spoilt, an only child of a doting father. But Jake could see no fault in her.'

'Did he tell you all this?' Davina asked.

'No. I had it in fact from a neighbour of theirs who knew Mum,' Georgina explained. 'Jake was mad to marry her. They became secretly engaged because she told him her father wouldn't let her marry till she was of age. On her eighteenth birthday Jake insisted they tell her father. She didn't want to, but he blurted it out to her father, who promptly threw him out of the house.'

'Why.'

'Because, it seems, madam had been leading Jake up

the garden path, but Daddy assumed Jake had taken advantage of her youth and innocence. She had a fiancé already. It was an arranged match and the man was much older than Linda, picked by her father, who was determined his daughter would marry a man as rich as she was herself, and someone who would care for her as she'd been used to at home. At that time, of course, Jake had nothing and was a nobody. As you know, his vast wealth is kept very quiet and was amassed much later. Well, Linda knew all about this marriage and was quite happy to wait for it, but in the meantime she amused herself with the local boys.'

'Jake must have been very hurt,' Davina whispered.

'He was, desperately hurt, especially in his pride, that Linda could have deceived him. He was pretty heavily disillusioned, and he's never been close to a woman since.' Georgina was wandering up and down the room. 'I know about all the ladies he squires around. Of course he's had women—he's attractive, wealthy, and he's a passionate man. But they're always a good deal older than Linda was and they all know the score. No one gets hurt when it's over, least of all Jake,' she sighed sadly, 'because Jake makes sure he's never involved . . . so you see, he wouldn't know how to handle things if he did . . . er . . . really find himself involved.'

For a moment neither of them spoke. Then Davina wondered if Georgina knew about Anita. She guessed not. A lot of things now made sense that had puzzled her— why Jake should love and want to marry someone so much younger. It was because he could prove to himself that a lovely, wealthy and young woman really wanted him for himself.

'Yes,' she said eventually, 'I see. Thank you for telling me. That makes sense of a lot I hadn't understood.'

'Good,' said Georgina with relief, 'and now whatever it is that's kept you apart. . . .'

'It doesn't change anything between us,' Davina interrupted hurriedly.

'Are you sure?'

'Yes, quite sure. And I don't really want to talk about it. Thank you for telling me. I'm grateful you told me, and it helps in a way. I can also understand your concern for Jake. But he and I . . . we don't have anything any more. What you . . . thought you saw downstairs is just a passing unimportant impulse for him. It means nothing.'

'. . . . And will I please mind my own business,' Georgina sighed. 'I get exactly the same from Jake, in less polite language when I try.'

'Oh, no, you haven't talked to him about me!' exclaimed Davina. 'Please, I beg of you Georgina, don't! If you have any affection for either of us, please don't. I really couldn't cope with that as well. . . .' Her voice broke and she knew she had given away her feelings to Georgina.

'Very well.' Georgina didn't turn round from the window. 'Don't get upset—I'll leave it. I know what a terrible mess well-meaning friends can make of things . . . it's just that I hate to see you both so unhappy. He's aged so much and looks so bitter, and you're so thin and pale. . . .'

Davina's voice was firm. 'I'm thin because I've been working very hard, and he may well be strained and worried because his father is ill.'

'You neither of you give an inch,' Georgina sighed wearily. 'Jake is almost a stranger now. Today is the first time we've seen him in months, and I know you've been avoiding us.' She turned round to face Davina. 'Perhaps I'm wrong. Maybe you are better apart to find other people with whom you can be happy.' She smiled. 'Let's leave it at that. Larry warned me not to talk to you about it, but you know me, I always like to have my say. Will you forgive me?'

Davina smiled a little tearfully. 'There's nothing to forgive. It's nice to have friends who care.'

As soon as she let herself out of the house she could smell the tobacco of Jake's cheroot. He was leaning smoking against the side of the car, his town Porsche this time and not the Rolls. Her heart sank. She felt quite unable to cope with him or with herself.

He threw away the cigar and straightened as she walked hurriedly to her own car. 'Are you ready to come to the hospital with me?' he asked, immediately behind her as she put the key into the door of her own car.

She tensed. 'I'm sorry, Jake.' She turned round to face him and opened her car door. He was unexpectedly much closer than she realised. 'I ... can't, I'm afraid,' she faltered and looked up into his face.

He moved suddenly and rather threateningly towards her, pushing her hard against the car so that she felt his breath on her face.

'Please, Jake,' she whispered. 'Georgina, Larry ... not here!'

'Very well,' he said coldly, 'come with me.' He gripped her arm tightly with one hand and took the keys from her with the other, locking her car and then marching her firmly towards the Porsche.

Inside the confines of the small sports car, Davina was overwhelmingly aware of him, his familiar aftershave cologne, the long legs, narrow hips and wide shoulders in the silk suit and the male tang of him that was uniquely Jake in her memory. In the bright afternoon sunlight he looked almost gaunt. She noticed his hands on the wheel, and there was no wedding ring, only the beautiful onyx she knew so well. She felt the aching emptiness and longing for him swamping her at his nearness, and she turned away to hide her face, looking out of the window.

'This isn't the way to St Thomas's,' she said suddenly.

'That's right.' His voice was clipped.

'Where are you taking me?' she demanded.

'Oh, do stop agitating, Davina, you're not about to be kidnapped.' His voice was impatient. 'I have to pick something up at my flat on the way.'

'No,' she didn't want to go back to his home with him, 'I can't! Look, Jake, you're making things difficult ... perhaps it would be better if I went to the hospital another time....' Her voice tailed off.

'Possibly,' Jake said briefly.

The rest of the journey was finished in silence and they drove down the ramp into the underground garage of his block of flats. The cool darkness hit her after the brilliant sunlight and she blinked nervously as he parked the car and got out. He came round to her side of the car and opened the door, but she didn't move.

'Come on, Davina, I haven't all night,' he said irritably.

'I'll wait here,' she said more firmly than she felt.

'You're coming upstairs,' he said flatly. 'Either you'll walk or I'll carry you.' He waited. 'Davina!' he intoned warningly.

She got out hurriedly. They walked to the lift and Jake unlocked the doors. They rode up to his flat in silence, not looking at each other. In the hall he left her.

'After that terrible champagne I need some coffee,' he flung at her, heading for the kitchen. 'Make yourself at home.'

The flat looked exactly the same. She remembered the night they had talked into the early hours and it felt like a lifetime ago. So much had happened and so much had changed since then.

'The coffee's percolating.' Jake appeared, taking off his jacket and loosening his tie. 'I'm just going to change out of these glad rags.' He avoided her eyes. 'Would you like a drink?'

'No, thank you,' she said stiffly.

He left the doors open and she could hear him moving about, opening drawers and banging cupboards. Her face flooded with colour as she imagined him changing.

She walked over to the window. There was a heat haze in the distance and the rooftops of London looked like a shimmering dream. There was something unreal, too, about her being here, she thought, after all this time, and she felt panic rising in her throat. She had to get out before he came back. She turned to the door.

'Here we are.' Jake put down the tray with two steaming mugs on a low table. 'We'll both feel better after this.'

He had changed into casual slacks with open-necked shirt, and Davina felt nervousness rising in her at his informal clothes.

He picked up one of the mugs and sank into the big leather armchair, totally relaxed. She took her own mug and sat down, gulping the hot sweet liquid.

'Are you happy?' he asked abruptly, still looking into his coffee.

'Er . . . yes, of course,' she said rather faintly.

'You don't look it,' he said harshly.

She wondered what he wanted of her. Why had he brought her up here? All she wanted was to get out of this flat so heavily loaded with memories.

'Can we go now, Jake?' she asked, and got up, putting down her coffee.

'Davina!' He was up and beside her in two swift strides, his arms gripping her shoulders, as he turned her round to face him. She refused to look up and gazed as if hypnotised at his smooth, brown neck where the buttons of his shirt were undone. 'Look at me.' His voice was thick.

She shook her head mutely. 'I want to go now, Jake.'

Neither moved, but his hands tightened on her until she flinched.

'Please let me go. You're hurting me,' she said quietly. He was breathing hard and she was suddenly afraid of him, frightened of his strength and his anger.

'Look at me, damn you!' He lifted her face with one hand under her chin, his fingers holding her throat, and she looked at him wide-eyed, her eyes swimming with emotion. His own were hard and silvery, and his body tense.

'Please, Jake, let me go,' she whispered, and closed her eyes to hide her tears from him.

'Do you know I could break your neck with one finger? Do you realise that? And do you know you're driving me to madness?'

He put his other hand to her hair, pulling her head back till she cried out loud with fear, tears falling from below her lashes down her cheek on to his hand.

'Oh, God, tears! I might have known it.' He loosened his hold slightly, but she was still imprisoned against him, unable to move away.

'Jake?' she asked. 'I don't know what you want. If that makes you angry, I'm sorry, but there's nothing I can do about it.'

He sighed. 'All right. Sit down.' He released her suddenly and pushed her down on to the sofa, standing over her, a staring, unseeing blindness in his eyes as he looked down at her. After an endless moment, he moved away to the windows.

'Davina,' he said heavily, 'why did you refuse to marry me?' His voice was cold.

Davina clenched her hands in her lap. 'Jake, why must we go over all this again? It's in the past and. . . .' She hesitated, afraid she was going to cry again.

'Why, Davina, I want to know?' he insisted. 'I know you wanted me. You still do . . . almost as much as I want you. I'm no boy—I can feel that. So why? Answer me!'

She spoke quietly into the silence.

'Because I couldn't marry without love,' she said simply.

'Yours or mine,' he asked evenly.

'Both.'

'And at that time . . . when I asked you . . . was there someone you loved, enough for marriage?'

The question hung in the air between them.

'Jake, I . . . won't go on with this question and answer game. You have no right to. . . . It's all over, and it's best left . . . please!'

He came back to stand over her, and she could feel the violence in him, barely held in check as he fought for control, his hands clenched into his pockets, his face set and grim.

'Davina, I'm warning you. I want an answer, and I won't be responsible for what I do next if you don't give me one. When I asked you to marry me, was there someone you loved?'

'Yes.'

'Was it Philip?' he shot at her.

She didn't look at him. 'No,' she said quietly.

Strangely she felt the tension in him ease, and she looked up. Their eyes met, and Jake's were deeply dark with pain and a bleakness she remembered seeing only once before, in the hall of his father's house. Her own unhappiness seemed to recede as she looked at him. She longed to comfort him, and instinctively she made a move towards him, holding out her arm. But at that moment he turned away from her and didn't see it. He put a hand wearily through his hair and straightened up.

'Very well,' he said at last. 'I'll take you back to your car.' His voice was indifferent.

Davina got up, trembling, giddy with emotion, tension tight in her throat. It was even harder to leave him this time. She longed to throw herself into his arms, uncaring whether he loved her. Instead she walked unsteadily to the door.

And then choice was taken away, as he moved and reached for her, pulling her into his arms. She made a feeble attempt to pull away, but his hands gripped her. As his head bent to hers, she knew she couldn't stop him a second time. She trembled at his nearness, the familiar heat spreading through her body at his touch. And then they were kissing, hungrily, longingly, their arms locked round each other as his mouth deepened possessively against hers. His hand went to her head, scattering the pins until her hair uncoiled and fell heavily down her back.

'Do you know how I've longed to do this?' He buried his face against her, trailing his fingers through her hair, breathing in her fragrance. He bent his head to kiss the hollow between her breasts as his hands caressed her, moving on her bare shoulders as he pushed aside her dress.

'Davina, I want you so. I don't care any more about

. . . anything else. Please let me make love to you. . . .'

She hardly heard him, conscious only of his hands and his mouth returning to her parted lips with increased passion. She felt him tremble against her as he pulled her softness tight to his hardened muscles, his hands on the smooth skin inside her dress. She didn't resist when he picked her up and carried her through the silent flat, her arms round his neck, her face buried against his shirt where she could feel the heat of his body and hear the hammering of his heart. Dimly she knew she would probably regret what she was doing because he didn't love her, but her mind was whirling into darkness, only her senses piercingly aware of her own need of him, her aching desire for him to love her completely, to belong to him as she had wanted to for so many endless nights.

He put her down on his bed, his eyes on her body, ardently, as if he could not stop gazing at her, till she felt suddenly shy and locked her arms round her breasts, the colour flooding her face.

'No,' he whispered urgently, 'don't hide from me . . . let me look at you. You're so beautiful, so much more than I ever imagined. . . .'

And then she was in his arms, his hard body warm and close against her, his lips and tongue finding nerve ends on her soft skin that roused her to a passion she would never have dreamed possible. She felt she was drowning, her longing for him at fever pitch, and she dug her fingers into the smooth, silky skin of his back, drawing him closer. She heard him groan as he crushed her body into the softness of the bed beneath him in a frenzy of wanting and needing.

'Jake,' she breathed, 'please, will you be gentle. . . .'

He stiffened into rigidity, and for an endless moment he was totally still. Then he rolled away from her and, in one swift movement swung himself off the bed, standing with his back to her.

The wrench was so terrible and unexpected, she just lay there, inert with shock, unable to move.

'Jake, what is it?' He didn't reply. 'Please,' she whispered, 'Jake, I don't understand . . . what's happened?'

'Leave it, will you, please, Davina?' His voice was ragged. There was a stony silence. Then he moved, reaching for a robe and belting it round him. 'Why didn't you tell me?' he said at last.

'Tell you what?'

'That you're still a virgin.'

'But . . . I thought you knew.'

'Oh, God, Davina, I never really believed. . . .'

'But what does it matter?' Davina said piteously.

'I don't play about with virgins,' he said harshly, his voice oddly strangled.

'Play about? Is that what it . . .?' Her voice tailed away into silence.

'Get dressed, Davina. I'll drive you home,' he said jerkily.

The door closed behind him and she was alone. She lay there unable to grasp what had happened. One moment Jake was blazing with passion and they were almost lovers, the next minute there was nothing, just an emptiness beyond tears.

She felt ice-cold and began to shiver, her body shaking uncontrollably. What had she done? Was it her lack of experience? Could he only enjoy making love to women who knew exactly what to do?

She had to get out before he came back. She didn't want him to take her home. She couldn't bear to see him again, ever. She felt a deep shame and humiliation at the wanton way she had shown him her love, her desire for him. Oh, God, what a nightmare!

She slipped off the huge bed and found her clothes on the floor. She dressed hurriedly, her fingers fumbling, unable to cope with the familiar movements. Finally dressed, she crept out into the corridor to the sound of water running—a shower. It sounded unnaturally loud in the hushed flat, and she prayed she could escape unseen. The living room was empty and she reached for her bag and coat. Stumbling out into the hall, she opened the front door noiselessly, letting it click quietly shut behind her. She ignored the lift and rushed down the stairs, holding tightly to the banisters to avoid tumbling headlong.

Dizzy and shaking, she reached the ground floor and ran out into the street, stunned to see it was still daylight. She seemed to have lived a lifetime in the last hour. She hailed a taxi and subsided into the dark interior, rigid with shock.

CHAPTER TEN

THE hospital smell hit her as she walked in through the main doors and asked the way to the ward. Following the signposts, she found it eventually, and the staff nurse asked her to wait.

'Mr Humphries has a visitor,' she said pleasantly, 'and we don't want to tire him. Sister has left orders that he's to have only one visitor at a time.'

'Oh,' Davina was suddenly terrified that Jake might be there after all. She had checked with his office and been told he was tied up with meeting until late.

'The lady has been with him some time, so it shouldn't be long to wait,' the staff nurse said cheerfully, and left Davina sitting on the hard vinyl bench in the corridor, voices and footsteps a blur around her.

She wondered again if it had been a mistake to come. She did want to see Jake's father, but what would they talk about? They had only one subject in common, and she could not imagine talking about Jake without giving herself away, letting him see her hurt and unhappiness.

It was only forty-eight hours since she had fled from Jake's bed. She had reached home and rushed up to her flat in panic and locked herself in, collapsing on the bed in a fit of weeping that left her weak and trembling.

The phone had rung incessantly, and Mrs Blunt had come come up several times to knock and call, but Davina had refused to answer. Eventually the ringing had stopped. She wondered if it had been Jake, but found it didn't matter. Nothing had mattered that night. She relived the afternoon with Jake, the moments of passionate intensity and the terrible humiliation of the end. Shame and disgust filled her when she thought about her own loss of control. She had almost begged him to make love to her, showing him all too clearly how she felt. And in the end he hadn't wanted her, not even physically.

Her only clear hope was that she would never have to see him again, that somehow she could walk out of his life once more and stay out of it for good.

Sunday she had stayed indoors, unable to sit still, wandering round the flat, her mind a blank and her body incapable of even the simple things of dressing and eating. On Monday morning she had finally emerged, eyes totally withdrawn, her face heavy with make-up. She went round to see Maddy, who was frantically busy, surrounded by ringing phones and knee-deep in crises.

'I've cancelled your job for the week and found a replacement,' said Maddy, far from pleased.

'Thank you.' Davina didn't know where to start explaining. 'And I'm sorry.'

They were not alone in the office. Maddy's secretary was handling clients and phone calls at the other end of the room.

'Maddy, I want a job abroad . . . anything, anywhere,' Davina said flatly, and Maddy looked at her intently.

'Do you want to talk about it?'

'No,' Davina said baldly.

Maddy's voice was cool and impersonal. 'You know I don't handle that kind of job, but I have plenty of mates with jobs abroad on their books.' She turned to Davina. 'How soon could you go?'

'Immediately,' Davina said evenly.

'Passport?'

'Yes, up to date.'

'Fair enough. I'll get on to it. Give me a ring this afternoon or first thing tomorrow. And now, love, if there's nothing else, I have to turf you out. There's rather a lot on today.' Maddy looked straight into Davina's eyes. 'You have my home number. If you want to ring me or see me this evening, I'll be home.'

'Thanks, Maddy. You're too good to me,' said Maddy with a catch in her throat.

'And for God's sake get yourself something to eat,' Maddy said roughly. 'You look ghastly!'

'Davina Richards! Well, well, well, what a surprise!' The voice was cool and faintly familiar.

Davina looked up at the elegant young woman in front of her. The corridor was crowded with nurses and trolleys and for a moment she didn't recognise the sophisticated brunette in a fashionable silk jersey suit, high-heeled sandals and a mink jacket draped over one shoulder, a frothy wisp of a chiffon hat on exquisitely cut black curls. It was Anita.

'Hello.' Davina's voice was cool.

'What are you doing here?' Anita cooed.

'Waiting to see Mr Humphries.'

'Senior or Junior?' Anita enquired archly.

'How is he?' Davina ignored Anita's last question.

'As well and depressed as can be expected, but I managed to cheer him a little. But I'm surprised to see you here. I rather thought you'd ... er ... severed your connections with the family.' Anita stared at Davina's ringless left hand. 'All that finished rather smartly, didn't it? Did you ever find that love we heard so much about last time we met?'

Davina flushed at the memory of her own outburst at their last meeting.

'Well, never mind,' Anita said consolingly, 'things don't always turn out as we expect, do they?' She sat down next to Davina in a rush of expensive perfume. 'Who would have thought that your hand would be ringless so soon and mine would carry the wedding ring?' She held out her left hand and showed Davina the glittering diamond with its matching white gold wedding ring.

Davina caught her breath. Anita and Jake were married! She felt the colour drain from her face, and the familiar giddiness take hold of her till she was certain she would black out. She closed her eyes and clenched her hands in an effort to avert a faint. After a moment the nausea passed and her throat eased slightly.

'My congratulations,' she said faintly.

'Thank you. How kind.' Anita's voice held a note of triumph. 'It all happened quite suddenly after that week-end when we met, you know. In fact it was so sudden for both of us, we haven't had time for a honeymoon, but now at last we're going and I shall have him to myself, cruising in the Caribbean. . . . Isn't that thrilling?' Davina said nothing. 'Any girl would envy me that, don't you think?'

Davina stood up. 'I must be going. I've been waiting to go in.'

'Oh, do hang on another minute.' Anita looked round. 'Jake should be here in a moment. He's picking me up. Do wait. I know he'll want to say hello . . . after all this time.'

Davina turned away. 'Excuse me,' she muttered, and forced herself to walk slowly up the corridor away from Jake's wife, determined the younger woman should not see her break down.

She turned the next corner, not caring where she went, only desperate to be out of sight of the girl Jake had married. Oh, God, how she envied her! This was the answer to that ghastly time in his flat. This was why he couldn't go through with their lovemaking. At the last moment he couldn't be unfaithful to his wife. She should have known. After all, she had been prepared for it.

Blindly she made for the nearest exit and walked in a daze out to the main road, where she flagged down a taxi.

'Paddington,' she directed him.

Home—that was what she needed. To go home where she could hide. The capital was no longer large enough to hold them both. The fear of running into Jake or having him track her down was now too great.

She thought fleetingly of luggage, of her car still at Georgina's, and found she didn't care about any of it. She would wait for the next train to Cornwall to take her home. A sense of relief swept over her at the thought of leaving London.

An hour later she was sitting in a crowded compartment of the Cornish Riviera Express, glad of the people and chat all round her, an escape from her own thoughts and problems. She spent the greater part of the journey in the dining car, over lunch and then back again for tea, grateful to the waiters who allowed her to linger while others came and went, and they cleared the debris of meals.

She watched idly as the congested urban housing gradually changed to the green of grass and crops. They travelled through a thunderstorm which brought a strange release to her own turbulent emotions. And then the shadows of animals in the fields lengthened and they were in Cornwall.

St Ives station was packed and bustling, in full season with holiday visitors. Davina debated whether to ring home and let her parents know she was on the way, but decided against it. It was almost dark when the taxi dropped her at the end of the road, anxious to return to more waiting customers.

As she opened the gate she noted her mother's roses in full bloom, a riot of yellows, pinks and oranges. Trepidation returned as she rang the bell. Had it been a mistake to drop in like this? The house was dark. Perhaps they were out?

She rang again and heard her father's voice.

'Hang on, I'm coming!' Relief gripped her throat as he opened the door, a newspaper in one hand. 'Ina!' there was no doubt of his happiness at the sight of her. He opened his arms and she went straight into them.

'My dear,' he said, 'what a surprise! Why didn't you let us know? Your mother's out, at Aunt Nancy's. She's not been too well.'

He held her at arm's length, looking at her face shadowed by the light of the hall lamp. There was a sudden silence as he saw her weariness, the dark shadows in her eyes and the pinched tension in her face. Davina looked away, unable to hold his gaze.

'It's good to be home,' she began lightly. 'I just came— I hope that's all right. A sudden urge to see you both, to be home for a bit.'

They turned and walked to the living room.

'Your mother will be over the moon,' her father said lightly, slightly selfconscious as he remembered their last meeting.

'London just seemed stifling,' Davina realised she was chatting about nothing, but couldn't seem to stop, 'and I felt I had to get away . . . from the weather, I mean, and the crowds.'

Her father stopped, 'What am I thinking of?' he exclaimed. 'you must be starving, you poor girl. What can I get you to eat?'

'Oh, no, I ate on the train, but I'd love a cup of tea.'

'Good,' he said turning to the kitchen, 'that gives me an excuse to have one.'

In the kitchen she watched him, sitting in her favourite position, elbows on the table, her face cupped in her hands.

'Er . . . no luggage?' he asked. 'It must have been sudden.' He turned round to face her. 'Er . . . is everything all right? Nothing wrong?' She looked away from him in slight confusion. 'Well, never mind' he went on, busy with cups and saucers, 'but I think I should tell you I've spoken to Jake Humphries . . . twice.'

'Oh, no!' the cry rang with suppressed emotion and he turned round. He looked at her for a moment, then came across to stand by her chair, stroking her hair as he used to do when she was little. She leaned against him.

'It's bad, isn't it?' he asked gently.

'Oh, Dad, it's all such a muddle! Please tell me why you talked to Jake.'

'Well, the first time was when I called your office to speak to you and was told you'd left, you weren't working there any more. I asked to speak to Jake and he confirmed that you'd left and that you and he . . . had decided to part.'

The silence was heavy and Davina forced herself to speak. 'I'm sorry, I should have let you know. Were you worried?'

'A little,' he said, and moved when the kettle began to whistle. 'Your mother more than I. She was all for rushing up to town to see you, but I persuaded her that you'd be in touch as soon as you wanted us to know what had happened.' He smiled at her, putting the hot tea on the table in front of her. 'And I was right—here you are. And now there's no rush. You tell us whatever you want in your own good time.' He sat down opposite her and stirred sugar into his cup.

'And the second time!' Davina asked.

'Last Saturday. Jake rang us. It seems he expected you to be here. He sounded upset when I told him we weren't expecting you.'

Davina looked down into her cup. So he had cared enough about her disappearance to try to find her. Just kind concern, she thought, nothing personal.

'Have you seen him?' her father asked.

'No, not really. By accident . . . we met at a christening. The baby of a mutual friend. Jake was godfather.'

Her father sighed. 'You know,' he said gently, 'I liked him.' He looked away from her deliberately. 'I know how badly I behaved to him that day, and the Sunday we had a drink at the club I went on at him in much the same way. But underneath I couldn't help liking him. He was loyal to you. He trusted you, where I hadn't. And he was right to be angry. I know now I got a lot of things wrong, and I hurt you and your mother. After the wedding, with Monica gone, I had time to think back, to remember and to wonder about things that hadn't struck me at the time. And now, with the baby coming, so soon. . . .' he stroked his chin slowly, in the way she knew so well, 'I think I jumped to some of the wrong conclusions, perhaps because I was hurt at the way you cancelled your wedding and left us in the lurch. Anyway, I'm not proud of the way I behaved. I had hoped some day I would have the chance to tell Jake, to explain. But at least I can tell you.' He looked at her. 'I'm sorry, child, and I hope what has happened had nothing to do with the things I said to you both.'

'No, Dad, nothing.' She put her face in her hands as the tears started, slowly, silently, and he moved his chair to sit beside her, cradling her head in his arms as he used to do. 'Dad, he's married. And I didn't know!'

Her father stiffened. 'You mean he was married that day when you were both here?' he demanded angrily.

'Oh, no, no, not then.' Her voice was muffled against his sweater. 'He married the girl next door. She's eighteen and has always adored him. And his father is thrilled. He'd always hoped for the marriage.' She was sobbing. 'I can't bear it . . . I love him so terribly.'

'Hush, child! It doesn't seem to make sense. How could he be married to his girl when he was engaged to you only . . . about two months ago?'

So Davina told him about Jake, leaving out only the emotional scenes with Philip on the beach and with Jake at his flat. That she could never tell anyone.

Her father didn't move until she had finished.

'I didn't want you and Mum to think I still loved Philip,' she ended.

'Well,' he said finally, 'life can get complicated, can't it? Ina, why did you refuse to marry him when he asked you? If you loved him?'

'Because he didn't love me. For him it was just a convenient arrangement and he . . . wanted me.'

'Are you sure?'

'Yes, of course I'm sure, ' Davina answered in surprise. 'He never mentioned love.'

'Men don't always, you know. It's something that's often more important to women.'

'Oh, Dad, that's not right! Didn't you mention love when you proposed to Mum?'

'That was different,' he said quietly, 'that was a different age.'

'I don't believe that. Anyway, I knew he didn't love me.'

'You don't think it might have come . . . later?'

Davina thought for a moment.

'He's used to a pattern of living with girl-friends who are changed regularly with the curtains and wallpaper. I think we could only have made a go of it if he'd really loved and wanted me. The kind of married arrangement he suggested left that out, completely.'

'Very well, dear. You know best, of course. Anyway, it's all over now he's married, so perhaps you were right about his feelings.'

'David, where are you?' It was her mother's voice. 'I'm back!' They heard the bang of the front door closing and then her mother stood in the doorway, mouth open, eyes wide in astonishment. 'Darling!' she cried, and Davina flew to hug her. 'What a lovely surprise! And I've nothing to eat. David, have you made her something? Oh, and your room ... the bed's not made up ... oh, why didn't you ring me at Nancy's, David, I would have come straight back. How long have you been here?'

Finally she stopped and her eyes moved to her husband's face across her daughter's head. He put his finger to his lips with a warning look.

Davina drew back. 'I ate on the train. And I can make my own bed, you know. I've come to stay for a few days ... is that all right?'

'Of course it's all right. I can't imagine anything nicer. And it doesn't matter about the bed or anything. I was just flustered for the moment. It's so lovely to see you.' Mrs Richards turned away to hide her tears at the sight of her daughter's unhappy face. She gave her coat to her husband. 'Will you hang that up for me, please, dear?' Her voice was thick with suppressed anger. 'And if Jake Humphries is the reason you look the way you do, then fiancé or not, I shall have words with him!'

'Oh, no, Mum, please!' Davina implored her. 'I couldn't bear it. Please, Dad!' she appealed to her father, and rushed out of the kitchen, upstairs to the little bedroom she had used the week-end of Monica's wedding.

Taking off her clothes, she picked a robe from the cupboard, had a quick wash and came back to creep into the unmade bed. Within minutes she was fast asleep.

She woke early and the house was quiet, as it had been each morning of the past week since she had come home.

She got up, pulled on sneakers, cord trousers, a fisher-
man's jersey and a duffle coat from the hall downstairs.
Quietly unlocking the kitchen door, she let herself out of
the house into the early dawn. It was damp and cool, and
she made for the dunes just as the sun rose hazily over the
distant headland.

She loved this time of day. There was not a soul stirring,
and she walked along the water's edge undisturbed, the
wet sand squelching under her feet, the wind in her face
and the gulls chattering shrilly overhead. Out at sea he
grey waters churned on to the horizon. During the past
week the turbulent beauty of this place she loved so much
had soaked into her, rebuilding her strength and reviving
her spirit.

The first morning she had phoned Maddy to say she'd
changed her mind about going abroad. Maddy had
accepted this without surprise, and suggested she get in
touch when she had decided what to do next.

In the days that followed Davina began to revive,
lapped round by her parents' love and care. They asked
no questions, made no demands. She could come and go
as she pleased, talk or not as she wished. She ate and slept
when she was hungry and tired at odd times of the day
and night, and they had not worried. She spent long hours
wandering along the beach, climbing the cliffs, searching
for shells, studying fish life in the rock pools and letting
her mind drift.

She thought about Jake, too, but differently. She loved
him, but he had married Anita, and this she had to accept.
She had been timid and unhappy long enough, and the
yearning and the dreaming had to stop. She knew she
would have to survive without him . . . somehow. She
didn't think she would ever marry, and she would always
be somewhere alone without him, her inmost self shut
away. But she would no longer whine for what she could
not have, because it belonged to someone else.

So she decided to go back to London. She would move,
and she would not live alone again. That kind of loneliness
was also over. She would find a flat to share with another

girl, and return to the world she loved ... advertising. She had ability and experience, and she should be able to get a job that would involve her, give her renewed self-respect and fill her life. When eventually she and Jake met again, as they were bound to do, she would be armoured, secure in a life of her own.

Suddenly a restless energy seemed to possess her, and she started running along the sands, her hair flying, her arms stretched high to the winds, the cobwebs in her mind dispersing.

Breathless, the colour vivid in her face, she arrived home to find her parents, sleepy and in dressing gowns enjoying an early cup of tea. Later, she thought, she would phone Maddy and tell her she was coming back to London ... to work and to live.

CHAPTER ELEVEN

THEY were dining at the Connaught. As she put the finishing touches to her make-up, Davina was conscious of a slight twinge. The Connaught was for ever imprinted on her mind as the place where she had breakfasted with Jake. But she put the thought away and counted her blessings. She looked good and she knew it. Her face had a new serenity, a quiet confidence that her job and her new boss had given her.

Toby Wyndham was a real star in the advertising world, running his own agency which was gradually winning interesting accounts from competitors. She had liked him immediately at the interview, and had been pleased when he had picked her from several more experienced applicants. She was his personal assistant, with a secretary of her own and an office on the first floor of the elegant house in Mayfair that was the Wyndham agency. It was much smaller than Foster Pattersons, and all the members of staff had to be prepared to turn their hand to anything that might come up. This had given her new confidence in her own ability, and Toby appreciated her dedication, her efficiency and her tact in dealing with people in a world notorious for difficult temperaments. He and his wife, Eileen, had drawn her into their social life, and she had blossomed in the happy atmosphere that Eileen insisted was essential for her husband's welfare. Elleen was an inspired hostess, and invitations to her dinner parties were much in demand.

Several times she had marvelled at Davina's resistance to the eligible, attractive bachelors who came her way and made no secret of their interest in the boss's P.A. But no one had pressed her. They all accepted that Davina was a very private person, and she returned each night with relief to the flat she shared with a friend of Maddy's just behind Lords cricket ground in St John's Wood.

Returning to London after that visit to her parents' home three months before, she had gone to see Maddy, who had helped her in a miraculously short time to find a job, a flat and a girl to share it with. Michelle was one of Maddy's temps, and led a hectic social life, so that they saw little of each other. They had each their own bedroom and shared kitchen, bathroom and a low-ceilinged, spacious attic sitting room which had been lovingly decorated and filled with personal possessions of both girls to make it comfortable and attractive. It was a good life, and Davina never took any of it for granted.

A dab of perfume and she was ready. The sea-green wild silk evening dress suited her tall, slender figure, flowing from a tight waist where a wide silver belt gathered the fullness of the low-cut top. Long transparent sleeves ended in large cuffs, and she wore satin pumps dyed to match. She was still a little thin, she observed critically, but the dress emphasised her long legs, and the colour showed up the silken heaviness of her coiled hair.

Tonight she was dining with the Wyndhams, largely to make up the numbers. One of the agency's American backers was here with his wife and brother, and Eileen and Toby were going to show them some of London's night life. Davina had met Mr and Mrs Winner at the agency earlier in the week, but Mr Winner's brother she only knew to be an attorney in the States. They were to meet for the first time that evening.

The horn from the mini-cab downstairs told her it was time to go. Speeding into the centre of London, she wondered again what miracle had prevented a meeting between herself and Jake. In the early weeks of her return from St Ives she had been afraid each day and every night that she might run into him. At the office she had expected to hear his voice on the phone, his name mentioned. The advertising world was not a large one and most people in it knew each other. But it had not happened.

She knew Toby was acquainted with Mark Foster of Foster Pattersons. They belonged to the same club and occasionally lunched together. But that seemed to be the extent of any contact between the two companies, and she prayed it would stay that way.

The mini-cab dropped her off at the entrance to the Connaught, and the driver bowed politely and drove off. It was one of Toby's most endearing qualities that he always organised transport for her when she was helping him to entertain clients in her own time. The others had just arrived when she joined them in the bar, and they settled down for drinks and a discussion of the menu.

Davina had a champagne cocktail which Toby set down before her within minutes of her arrival. She raised her glass and thanked him with a smile. She always picked a light meal on these occasions, and settled on a consommé followed by grilled sole and salad. When everyone had chosen and Toby had ordered, the conversation began. Davina sat back and looked at her companion for the evening. Bill Winner was a tall, rangy Texan around thirty-five, she guessed. His hair was bleached blond and curly, his eyes blue, with laughter and sun lines around them. He was expensively dressed in the American style, and his glances told her he appreciated what he saw. They were soon engaged in light, amusing conversation and Davina knew she was going to enjoy the evening. He took her arm lightly as they made their way to the restaurant and made sure he was seated by her.

Davina looked around and heaved a sigh of relief. At night the busy and crowded restaurant bore no traces of the hushed, sunlit breakfast room she remembered. Bill Winner smiled at her, one eyebrow raised in query as he leaned towards her.

'Ghosts?' he asked.

'How did you guess?' she countered.

'I must make sure they're well and truly laid during the evening, then.' He lifted his glass. 'To my stay in London,' he said in mock solemnity. 'May the rest be as enjoyable as this moment.'

Davina laughed with pleasure at his nonsense and the talk round the table became general as the first course appeared.

Coffee was being poured when she felt a strange tingle down her back, as though she was being observed. She shook herself slightly to dismiss the fancy and concentrated on the photographs of his wife and children that Bill Winner was spreading for her on the table.

'Now this was last summer when. . . .' He stopped suddenly. 'Are you cold?'

Davina smiled. 'No, just someone walking over my grave, I think,' she said lightly. 'Go on.'

He leaned back in his chair. 'It's none of my business,' he said quietly and more seriously than she had yet seen him, 'but there's someone sitting at the far end of the room behind you who's been watching you for some time.'

Davina stiffened. Could this be it? Would this be the evening and the place where she would run into Jake and Anita? A sudden fear clutched at her, and her throat tightened as it hadn't for many a day.

But then she lifted her chin. She couldn't spend the whole of her life dreading this encounter. Perhaps it would be easier once it was over. She smiled at her companion.

'That accounts for it, then,' she said brightly. 'Please go on.'

'Well, this holiday was rather funny. . . .' He looked up unexpectedly to catch sight of the rigid set of her face. He leaned forward and took one of her hands lying on the table and clasped it in his. It was warm and firm and, for a moment, Davina clung to him.

'You think you know who it is. Is that right?' he asked gently. She nodded. 'Right,' he said quietly, 'let's take it from there. You just sit quietly and hang on to me. I'm going to describe him to you.' He paused to look at her intently. 'Are you ready?'

'Yes.'

'OK., here goes. He's a big fellow—very big, tall, broad and sort of rugged, dark hair, straight, I think. He's in evening dress. He's looking over at us and he can see I'm holding your hand. He looks kind of serious. Attractive, I would guess, to the womenfolk.' He turned his eyes back to her to see a glimmering of tears on her lashes. 'It's him?' he asked.

Davina nodded again and swallowed hard.

'Right,' said Bill, and turned to a passing waiter. 'Would you bring me a Cointreau, please?'

'Not for me, I hope. . . .' Davina began.

'Now let me tell you something, young lady,' he interrupted. 'I have years of experience of emotional females. I live with two. My wife is so soft, even watching our kids at the dentist makes her cry, and my four-year-old daughter is a collector of strays—animal and human, which is going to be a lifelong trial to us all.'

Davina smiled tremulously at that.

'Let me tell you about Cointreau,' Bill went on. 'It's light, not intoxicating, and guaranteed to lift the morale. Take it from me. It works even with my wife.'

The waiter put the clear liqueur down in front of him.

'Here we are,' Bill Winner said cheerfully; and pushed it over to her. 'Now I'm going to watch you drink it.'

'Do you always announce what you're going to do before you do it?' she asked.

'Invariably with females in shock, yes. I've found it works wonders. Now drink it, and I mean all of it.'

Davina drank and felt the soothing liquid melting the constriction in her throat.

'Breathing better?' he asked.

'Yes.'

'Good. Now your young man isn't going to come over here and say hello. If he'd planned that he would have done so by now. That means. . . .'

'He's not my young man,' Davina protested.

'Well, it's none of my business, but it looks to me, if he's not your young man, he wants to be just that. Anyway, he's not going to accost you in the restaurant. So there's no need to worry there might be a scene. I would guess it's far more likely he'll send you flowers in the morning and it will all come all right.'

She bowed her head at that and looked down at her hand, still firmly in his grasp.

'Forgive me,' he said as he leaned towards her. 'I'm a silly blundering fool. Take no notice.'

She shook her head, striving for composure.

'Davina,' Eileen leaned across the table, 'we're just saying we've been here long enough. Toby wants to go on to Annabel's. Are you about ready to move?'

'Yes, of course, Eileen. It's been lovely.'

'Good.' Eileen turned to her husband. 'Shall we go, darling?'

'Right-ho. You ladies collect your wraps and we'll follow.'

Bill Winner let go of her hand, and the men stood as the ladies left the table. Davina kept a tight control on herself and did not turn round to look for Jake. In the cloakroom she sat thankfully and repaired her make-up, listening only vaguely to the chat of the two older women. Retrieving their coats, they moved back into the foyer, and Davina stopped, frozen, as she saw Jake and Mark Foster in conversation with Toby and the Winners.

'Are you all right?' Eileen touched Davina's arm. 'You look a bit pale suddenly, dear.'

Davine shook herself slightly. 'Yes, of course, I'm fine, thank you,' and she smiled at the other woman.

'Darling,' it was Toby pulling Eileen forward, 'I don't think you've met Jake Humphries, who works with Mark.'

Davina kept in the background while introductions were made all round, and looked at Jake for the first time since she had run from his flat and his bed. She had forgotten how tall he was, how broad in the shoulders, and how magnificent he looked in evening dress. His face seemed less tanned and the shadows round his eyes looked almost black. She remembered fleetingly his father speaking of insomnia, and wondered if it was worse. His face was set into the grim lines she knew so well. He smiled formally down at the ladies, then looked up unsmilingly straight into her eyes.

'Davina, what a delightful surprise!' It was Mark Foster coming towards her with outstretched hands. 'So you were the lucky one she went to, Toby. You never mentioned it before.' He took both her hands in his and bent to kiss her cheek. 'Beautiful as ever,' he went on, then turned to Jake. 'Aren't you sorry you let her go?' he quizzed.

'How are you, Mr Foster?' she said quietly, as he let go of her and moved away. 'How is Mrs Foster?'

'Very well, thank you, very well.'

Toby laughed. 'Don't think you're going to tempt her back, Jake, will you? Because I won't let her go. I think the place would collapse without her now.'

'Well, this has been nice.' Mark Foster drew back. 'We mustn't keep you.' He turned politely to Mrs Winner. 'I hope you enjoy the rest of your stay in London.'

During the ensuing goodbyes, Jake moved towards Davina and she felt an urge to flee. But she controlled herself and stood her ground, giving him a cool smile as he came up.

'You look well, Davina.' His voice was cold and controlled.

'Thank you, Jake. How are you?'

He ignored her question. 'Have you been with Toby Wyndham long?' he asked harshly.

'About two months now.'

'Are you enjoying it?'

'Very much, thank you.'

He smiled sardonically and she said nothing, but started to move away.

'Davina. . . .' He put out a hand towards her and she flinched back instinctively, terrified of his touch. She heard the hiss of his indrawn breath and looked up to see his eyes blaze with anger and something else she couldn't quite identify. A moment later the emotion had gone and his face was shuttered as he looked down at her, his eyes expressionless and curiously dead.

'Jake?' she prompted.

She thought he was about to speak, but just then Bill Winner came up to her and, drawing her arm through his, nodded at Jake in a friendly manner.

'We have to be on our way. It's good to have met you.'

Within minutes they were on the pavement outside, stepping into two cars waiting to take them on for the rest of their evening.

The following day Davina spent in a daze, moving mechanically through her work, apprehensive at each ring of her phone in case it was Jake. But he did not ring, and she found she was wavering between relief and disappointment. She told herself fiercely not to be stupid, and left the office promptly to rush home. Relieved to find a note from Michelle to say she would be away for the night, she changed into her favourite pale pink towelling robe, brushed her hair and settled in front of the fire, her feet drawn up under her on the sofa. She breathed in the scent of the yellow roses that had arrived from Bill Winner and found them strangely comforting.

Well, the first encounter was over, and she hoped it was the worst. It seemed terrible to have to admit that nothing had changed in her feelings for him. Last night she had wanted him to take her away from everyone, she had longed again to be in his arms close to him, and she had wanted him to love her as she still loved him. How much longer could this go on? Perhaps she could throw herself into an affair with someone else. Should she finally accept some of the many invitations she had turned down over the past months, knowing they would all lead to the same inevitable end, an end she had not wanted? Maybe that way lay forgetfulness. Perhaps with someone else she could finally erase the memory of Jake from her mind and heart?

She sighed and got up restlessly. Coffee and some television, she decided, and she was in the kitchen when the doorbell rang.

Damn, she thought, someone for Michelle again. Let them ring! She was in no mood to see anyone. She tiptoed into the living room with her coffee hoping they would go away, but the bell went on ringing. Someone seemed to have their finger on it. She was furious when she finally opened the door.

'Well?' she demanded belligerently. It was Jake.

She stood looking at him, mesmerised, unable to believe her eyes.

'How did you find me?' she asked at last, her voice nervous and high-pitched.

'Through Maddy,' he said calmly, looking her over from her loose hair, down the belted dressing gown to her bare feet.

Her face flamed at his glance, and anger fought with the elation she felt at the sight of him.

'What is it you want, Jake?' she asked woodenly. 'I'm busy.'

'Yes, I can see you are,' he drawled. Can I come in?' Perhaps it was the quickest way to get rid of him she thought. 'Oh, very well, come in. But make it quick, whatever you want.'

He walked past her into the sitting room. 'This is cosy,' he remarked, and shed his leather coat. Flushing, Davina looked away from the muscled thighs clad in tight black trousers, and the wide shoulders under the fine cream sweater that emphasised the crisp blackness of his hair.

'Well,' she said evenly, 'what do you want?'

'Aren't you going to ask me to sit down?' he asked.

'No.'

They stood facing each other. It was Davina who lost her cool.

'If you want me to come back and work for you, the answer's no,' she said heatedly.

'The thought never crossed my mind,' he said mildly, towering over her, making the low room feel hot and close.

'Oh, for God's sake, sit down!' she snapped crossly.

'Thank you,' he said meekly. 'What an irresistible invitation.' His eyes wandered round the room and then he saw the roses. His mouth hardened. 'Ah, roses ... the flowers from last night's admirer. For services rendered, I suppose,' he said harshly.

Davina stiffened with anger.

'I'd like you to go now, Jake. Nobody talks to me like that, and I don't have to take it from you!'

He got up, reached for his coat and made for the door. In the tiny hall he turned back.

'Davina,' he said huskily, 'I want to stay—please! I need to talk to you.'

She looked up at him. His eyes seemed to be pleading with her, almost begging her. She didn't understand what this was about, but she couldn't turn him away if he needed her.

'I'll just go and change,' she said.

'No,' he said urgently, 'don't go. Please.'

'Coffee, then?' she asked.

'No, thanks.'

She sat down and waited. Jake walked about the room, finally standing in front of the window, his hands in his pockets, looking out.

Davina swallowed hard. 'How is Anita?' she asked carefully.

'Anita?' he echoed, astonished. 'She's fine.'

The silence resumed. The room was darkening, and she could see only the shape of him at the window, the set of his head, his hands thrust deep into his pockets. She wondered what he was thinking.

'Does it ever seem strange to you, Davina,' he asked, his voice low, 'that we worked together for almost two years, amicably and successfully, and then in one week-end that just went, disappeared.' She sat still, half afraid of what was to come. 'Do you remember that evening in my flat, the night before we went to Cornwall when we talked into the early hours?'

'Yes.'

'It seems so long ago, and yet it's only a tiny slice out of my life, just a few months since that day. And nothing has ever been the same, will ever be the same again. You try so hard to fill your life ... work, travel, other women. And all the time you kid yourself, but you go on. You build a front, you believe in it. Maybe t's all going to be all right. And then in one moment it just collapses to dust. Last night there you were, so beautiful, so remote and so familiar, and everything I'd built up over the months just crumbled to ashes.'

He put a hand wearily to his head. 'All I could think about was you. All I could see was your face, your body. Every curve of your body is indelibly engraved on my memory. It's all I can see when I try to sleep, when I try in vain to make love to other women. And then that damn Yank at your side,' his voice was suddenly harsh, 'his hands on you, and all I wanted was to throttle him, and take you away somewhere where only I could touch you. . . . Oh, God, it's pathetic, isn't it? Do you know, Davina, there are times when I feel my love for you is a kind of madness and that I'm truly losing my sanity.'

She sat thunderstruck. What was he saying? He loved her? Had done for months? Impossible. He'd married Anita, how could he love someone else? Perhaps this was a joke or some kind of revenge for the day when she ran away.

'How dare you come here and tell me you love me! If that's what you want to talk about, I don't want to hear it. It means nothing to me . . . nothing!' Her voice was rising, her breathing heavy. 'Go and tell your wife. You don't make love to virgins—well, I don't sleep with married men. If that's what you came for, you're wasting your time. And now get out of here before I say something I'll really regret.'

'What are you talking about?' he thundered at her. 'I know you don't want my love—God knows you've told me often enough. And I know I'm too old for you. That, too, I've been told repeatedly. But don't go off into one of your dreams with me, girl. Wife? What wife? I have no wife. The only woman I want for wife doesn't want me.'

There was a sudden shattering silence in the room. They faced each other now as the tension stretched to breaking point. Jake's hands were tightly clenched at his sides, his mouth drawn into a thin line, his eyes blazing.

'Anita,' whispered Davina. 'Anita ... you and she are married. She told me.... Jake, I don't understand.'

She swayed and put a hand behind her to find the sofa. Before she could move he was beside her, his hands gripping her arms till she flinched.

'What are you babbling about, Davina? You thought I was married ... to Anita?'

'Yes. I saw her ring ... she told me....'

'Anita is married, but not to me,' he growled at her now, and his arms tightened. 'I want to know why you thought it was to me.'

She looked at him, unable to grasp what was happening. He loved her. He wasn't married to Anita. Could it be true?

'Answer me, woman, before I do you an injury!' The anger in his face was frightening.

'I don't know, Jake. She showed me the ring and she said I was the one who hadn't a ring and she had ... she said she was waiting for you, at the hospital. ...'

'So you jumped to the conclusion she was married to me.' His eyes glittered and his voice was a sneer. 'I remember that day. Anita told me she'd seen you. And it was just two days after you and I had been together at my flat ... in bed. And you think I could make love to you like that if I was married?' He let go of her suddenly and she fell back on to the sofa. 'No wonder you don't love me if that's what you think I am!' He walked away from her. 'It's all hopeless, isn't it? I should never have come.' He picked up his coat. 'Well, this evening has achieved one thing,' he smiled grimly. 'You won't be bothered by me ever again. In future if we meet I'll keep my distance.'

'Jake!' Her cry stopped him. 'Please wait!' She couldn't get the words out through her constricted throat, and he hesitated as he saw her struggle with her emotions.

'I love you' she said at last in a low voice. 'I have ... for months. ...'

'Spare me, Davina,' he said cuttingly. 'I don't need

your pity. I would never settle for that, so you can forget it.'

'Oh, no, Jake, it's true! Oh, God, how am I going to convince you? I love you. That's why I left Foster Pattersons. I couldn't bear to be with you, close to you, in case you guessed.' She stopped and waited.

'Then will you tell me why you refused to marry me? Why you told me there was someone else you loved for whom you turned me down?'

'When you proposed it sounded like a . . . a sort of arranged marriage of convenience. You talked about entertaining and having children, and the way you described it I thought you just wanted. . . .' Her voice sank to a whisper. 'I couldn't have lived a cold-blooded marriage with you because I loved you too much. I wanted so much more than you offered . . . and then later, when you asked me, all I said was that there was someone I loved. I didn't say someone *else*. It was you!'

Jake suddenly stilled, standing motionless, looking down at her. She watched his face, her own wet with tears.

'Cold-blooded? Not love you? Oh, dear God! I'm mad about you, insanely, crazily in love with you. . . .'

Davina watched the tension leave his eyes, and he opened his arms to her. She flew to him and he was kissing her frantically, her eyes, her temples, her hair, holding her close as she wavered between laughter and tears. 'I can't believe it,' he groaned. 'It can't be true.' He kissed her lips, parting them fiercely with his own, moulding her body to his as though he couldn't bear to be separate from her any longer. And she kissed him back, passionately, releasing the pent-up emotions of months without him.

He picked her up and sat down with her on his lap, holding her tight, running his hands through her hair, murmuring her name.

'Oh, Davina, I must have you . . . and soon. When will you marry me? Please make it soon.'

'As soon as you like,' she breathed, suddenly shy.

She lifted her hands to the heavy crisp hair, pulling his head down to hers and giving him her first kiss, long and sweet. Jake gasped his pleasure as she moved her hands down his back and under his sweater, caressing the smooth muscled skin.

'We must be sensible,' he whispered huskily. 'My dearest girl, please!'

'Must we?'

'Definitely,' he said, ruffling her hair and pushing her gently from him, 'but not for long—that I promise you.' He spoke joyously, a new note of possessiveness in his voice. 'I want you for my wife a week from today. Will you, my darling, without fuss or ceremony, in a small church somewhere?'

'Yes, Jake,' she breathed shyly, 'yes, please!' She sat up, suddenly serious. 'Jake, that day at your flat . . . why did you . . . leave me?' she asked painfully.

Contrition was in his eyes as he pulled her roughly back into his arms. 'I've been so ashamed about that. I wanted you so desperately, and yet I knew there was a man you loved. You'd told me so, remember? I felt I had to have you, whoever you loved and wherever you went to afterwards. Then, when I discovered I was the first, I knew I couldn't go through with it. I could never have let you go afterwards to anyone else. So I had to pull back. I couldn't have survived losing you if I'd made you mine.' He spoke grimly, holding her so tight, she could barely breathe. 'It was better to let you go to someone else without having you first.' He buried his face in her neck. 'Can you understand that?'

For a while there were no words for either of them.

'When did you know you loved me, Jake?' Davina asked next.

'I was almost sure that evening when you came here and talked to me about yourself. But I'd never felt like that before about anybody, and I wasn't sure. I just didn't want to lose you, to go back to our past relationship, and that's why I suggested. . . .' His voice tailed off as he kissed the tip of her nose.

'Go on,' she demanded.

'I was sure at Cartiers. As soon as I saw my ring on your finger, I knew it belonged there, and I wanted you to wear it always. And then over the week-end I suffered the most grinding jealousy. I'd never felt it before, and I just couldn't handle it. Every time you were with Philip or looked at him I imagined you were planning an affair with him after his marriage.' He sat rather grimly, thinking into the past. 'My reason and my knowledge of you just flew out of the window.' He crushed her to him with sudden fierceness. 'Oh, God, I couldn't go through it again. You won't ever leave me, will you?'

Davina looked at him wonderingly. The great Jake Humphries, begging her not to leave him? And yet she knew exactly how he felt, because she had gone through much the same thing.

'I felt the same about Anita,' she said slowly.

'Anita?' he asked. His voice hardened. 'Did my father talk to you about his favourite fairy story, that Anita and I would get married?'

She looked at him in surprise.

'Oh, yes, I know all about it,' he assured her. Anita had a crush on me when she was a schoolgirl, and my father was so desperate to marry me off to anybody he built up this fantasy that I loved her, but was too scared to tie her up while she was so young. Well, none of that was the truth. When I kissed her that day when we arrived . . . well, I was trying to make you jealous, and I hoped I was putting you through some of the same that I'd been suffering.' He laughed. 'Did it succeed at all?'

'You know it did,' she said, 'only too well. When she showed me her wedding ring, I was completely convinced it was you.'

'No chance. She had no intention of marrying me. She wanted someone who would dance attendance on her, not a man who had to work for his living. And she found it . . . and good luck to her. But that day she lammed into you I told her a few home truths.'

'Did you hear us . . . I wasn't sure how much you'd heard,' she said uncertainly.

'Well, neither of you was exactly quiet, you know,' he smiled reminiscently, 'but I wasn't having her talk to you as she did. And when you'd finished with her I told her to stop fantasising about marriage with me, that I was marrying you and she'd better accept it. She was furious.' He kissed her lightly on her eyes. 'But what intrigued me was hearing from the woman I loved what her ideas were on love and marriage. I've remembered that . . . and I shall certainly hold you to it.'

Davina giggled, 'Yes, I did rather lay it on, didn't I? I was so angry!'

'That was obvious!'

'What about my father?' she asked next, rather anxiously. 'That was such an awful part of the week-end.'

'Yes—well, he made me very angry. He also made me realise I was too old for you.' He turned to look into her face. 'Davina. . . .'

'Hush!' she interrupted, putting her hand over his lips.

'Do you know how old I am?' Jake persevered.

'I've never given it a thought.'

'I'm thirty-seven. In three years I'll be forty.'

'So you will, my darling. When is your birthday?' Davina smiled at him.

'You're a minx,' he said, 'and I'm besotted with you.'

'Tell me how you got on with Maddy,' she said, nestling close to him, ecstatic that there would be no more partings.

'Mm . . . well, that was a bit underhand. After last night I knew I had to see you. My one hope was that you wore no ring on your left hand, that you weren't committed to another man. So this morning I sent to Personnel for your file, and I saw that we'd appointed you through Madeleine Bell. I thought she might know where you were.' He smiled down at her happily. 'So I went to see her today.'

'You could have rung me at the office, at work,' she told him.

'Oh, yes, I could, of course,' he gibed playfully, 'and can you imagine the welcome I would have had? The cool, efficient Davina Richards turning me down on the telephone, firmly, definitely.' He flicked a finger at her cheek. 'I couldn't risk it. He smiled down at her happily. 'Seeing Maddy was very enlightening,' he teased.

Davina sat up indignantly. 'If Maddy told you. . . .'

'She didn't tell me anything,' Jake interrupted. 'She asked me a lot of questions and looked at me and smiled rather secretly several times. Anyway, we got on famously, and I told her if you turned me down, I'd come back and marry her.' He laughed as Davina pummelled him with her fists and they fell down on top of each other on to the sofa.

'You do know,' he said, suddenly grave, 'I'm going to be a very demanding husband? I want you in my bed every night, at my breakfast table every morning. I'm so longing to sleep in the same bed with you all night, night after night . . . oh, God, it's going to be a long week. No more sleepless nights without you beside me after we're married, my girl. And I want you with me everwhere, when I travel, when I entertain, all the time. I don't know if I can share you with a career. How do you feel about that?' he asked rather anxiously.

'I have my own worries, too,' Davina confided. 'How will you feel about . . . being married? You're used to change. How are you going to manage with just me?'

Jake sat up and pulled her to sit beside him, holding both her hands in a firm clasp. 'There can never be anyone else for me. Not ever. Not again. You'll understand your hold on me once we're married. And I want to be alone with you for a time—no children right away, not until you feel deep in your heart and your very bones my unending need of you. Then you'll know that your body, your love and your sweetness are my complete fulfilment.' He looked deeply into her eyes. 'I only hope and pray, my dearest girl, I can be the lover to bring you happiness and fulfilment in the same way.'

'Oh, Jake!' she whispered, and flung herself into his arms.

Harlequin Plus

THE BEAUTY OF CORNWALL

As a romantic setting for a Harlequin novel, Cornwall has, perhaps, few equals. A rugged peninsula stretching into the Atlantic Ocean, Cornwall is the most southwesterly county of England. Its miles of narrow, winding coastal roads are punctuated by centuries-old fishing villages and sandy coves that nestle between steep rugged cliffs. Despite the high seas that often lash the coastline ferociously, particularly at the extreme tip, Land's End, Cornwall has a relatively warm climate that encourages tourists to visit, writers, artists and artisans to settle there, and even a few palm trees to flourish!

Cornwall is the land of the ancient Celts, with a romantic and colorful history dating to pre-Christian times. It was the holy men from Ireland who came to convert the Cornish to Christianity, and the ancient stone crosses found in Cornwall today are relics of those days. Many medieval castles and monastic structures still remain intact. St. Michael's Mount, a onetime Benedictine monastery, is a breathtaking sight, rising from the ocean on a lofty granite crag off the coast by Penzance.

Smugglers, pirates, rumrunners and scheming scavengers of the sea are all part of Cornwall's more recent history, and in the village pubs local inhabitants are likely to regale the visitor with exciting stories of these bygone days.

Inland away from the roar of the ocean, Cornwall is peaceful and serene, her heathery moorlands dotted with old stone churches and small dairy farms. One of the products of these farms is the famous thick Cornish cream—a must with strawberry jam and fresh-baked scones at any number of local charming tea shops.

FREE!

A hardcover Romance Treasury volume containing 3 treasured works of romance by 3 outstanding Harlequin authors...

... as your introduction to Harlequin's Romance Treasury subscription plan!

Romance Treasury

... almost 600 pages of exciting romance reading every month at the low cost of $6.97 a volume!

A wonderful way to collect many of Harlequin's most beautiful love stories, all originally published in the late '60s and early '70s. Each value-packed volume, bound in a distinctive gold-embossed leatherette case and wrapped in a colorfully illustrated dust jacket, contains...

- 3 full-length novels by 3 world-famous authors of romance fiction
- a unique illustration for every novel
- the elegant touch of a delicate bound-in ribbon bookmark... and much, much more!

Romance Treasury

... for a library of romance you'll treasure forever!

Complete and mail today the FREE gift certificate and subscription reservation on the following page.

Romance Treasury

An exciting opportunity to collect treasured works of romance! Almost 600 pages of exciting romance reading in each beautifully bound hardcover volume!

You may cancel your subscription whenever you wish! You don't have to buy any minimum number of volumes. Whenever you decide to stop your subscription just drop us a line and we'll cancel all further shipments.